IN SEACH OF SANDINO'S GOLD

A TONY TAYLOR ADVENTURE

BOB MEANS

High Tide
Publications, Inc.
It's never too late to write

Deltaville, VA

Published by High Tide Publications, Inc.
www.Hightidepublications.com

Thank you for choosing this authorized edition of *In Search of Sandino's Gold*.

At High Tide, our mission is to discover, promote, and publish the work of talented authors over 50. Your support by purchasing an authorized copy is crucial in helping us bring their work to you.

Your support in our mission to bring the work of our authors to a wider audience is deeply appreciated. Thank you for choosing to purchase an authorized edition.

Edited by Carol J. Bova.

Book design by Firebellied Frog Graphic Design
www.Firebelliedfrog.com

ALSO BY BOB MEANS

My Soul to Keep, a Marine's Journal After Combat

Stealing Chili Relleno

The Adrian Account

This book is dedicated to Hal Moore
One of the last true journalists,
he passed away in December 2023.
A great friend we'll all miss.

AUTHOR'S NOTES

In the late 1950s and early 1960s, Fidel Castro's Cuban revolution ignited revolutionary fervor throughout Latin America. The Order of Jesuit Priests and their Liberation Theology inflamed Central America.

The people you will meet in the story are real people, including Santiago. Names have been changed for their protection.

Santiago was born in Nicaragua in the 1950s. He was a hateful and bitter man. Raised dirt poor, the youngest in a family of ten children, he watched his siblings struggle to put food on the table.

His father, a constant drunk, caroused until the early morning in bars and brothels, spending his children's earnings.

His sisters turned to prostitution to support the family. They came home early in the morning, bloodied and bruised by aggressive clients who used them for their twisted, deviant sexual fantasies.

Santiago's devout Catholic mother offered him to the Church as an altar server. He was sexually abused by one of the priests.

Anger burned deep in Santiago's soul. While an altar server, a visiting Jesuit priest took him aside, befriended him, and became the father figure he'd never known. The priest taught him liberation theology and told him of Castro and the struggle in Cuba. The priest found a place for him at the University of Leon and worked a way for him to go to Cuba and join Castro.

While he fought with Castro to appease his hatred and anger, he took on the grizzliest tasks — assassinated industrial leaders, organized firing squads, and joined the front lines of any military operation. He killed to feed the fire of hate that burned in his gut. He felt honored Castro appointed him to return to Nicaragua to reignite Augusto Sandino's revolution in his own country.

Santiago had the experience to accomplish this assignment. His first task was to find a hidden cache of gold lost for years. The location of Sandino's gold was fuel for the revival of the Sandinista dream in Nicaragua.

In this story, our protagonists, Tony Taylor and his best friend Lefty Jackson, are assessed as they travel to Nicaragua with an Australian boxer to find easy riches. They are oblivious to the political realities and the web of intrigue that captures them. Once they arrive, confronting Santiago, a seasoned revolutionary, takes more than a little effort.

CHAPTER 1

Born in San Francisco, at 23, I took after my dad with his ruddy complexion and tight body. And, like my dad, I smiled out of the corner of my mouth.

My father made a lot of money in Navy sheet metal contracts during the Second World War and invested it in California oil. He started a family trust fund, and through that, I lived a carefree life in San Francisco until November 10th, 1964, when my life changed forever.

A north salty breeze rushed off the bay, chilling the downtown streets as I sat alone in the cozy bar of Tony Nik's Cafe in North Beach. I came here every Thursday to meet up with my old school chum, Lefty Jackson, to swap our latest encounters as Male escorts. Light showered the bar from a curved, block glass window in front of the building.

I pulled a pack of Camels and a Zippo lighter from my black leather jacket. I reached with my lips to take out a cigarette and struck the Zippo to light it up. I took a deep drag and exhaled through my mouth and nose.

Thick smoke swirled around as I set the Zippo on the pack next to my Jack Daniels on the rocks.

Aggravated Lefty wasn't on time, I nursed my drink and checked my watch. It was a quarter after three.

Lefty, with his thin face, dark shades, straggled goatee, and head on a painfully bony body, finally opened the front glass door and came to the bar. He unzipped his black leather jacket, put his shades on top of his black hair, and slid onto the stool beside me.

I held up my watch, "You're late."

He nodded, grunted at me, put his elbows on the bar, rubbed his face, reached over, took out one of my Camels, lit it with my Zippo, and tossed it back in front of me.

"Anything else I can get for you?" I asked sarcastically.

"No, you're doing just fine," he said, exhaling through his nose.

Jim, the barkeep, placed a coaster and napkin in front of Lefty and set down a Coors. He knew us well.

Lefty looked into Jim's squinty eyes above a pencil-thin mustache. He raised his drink in appreciation, then chugged down half the bottle.

"I was late because I was on the phone with this crazy chick," he said, gulping down the rest of the bottle.

"How crazy?" I asked as Jim opened another beer with the opener that hung on his alligator belt.

"Pretty crazy. You know her. She's that plump chick who wears blue lipstick."

"Oh her. Yeah, she's pretty crazy. What'd she want this time?" I rattled the ice cubes in my glass.

"She wanted me to dress as a girl and go shopping with her on Market Street."

I sipped the last of my Jack Daniels.

"What did you tell her?"

"I told her to forget it. She could find someone down in the Castro."

While we talked, a short guy in his mid-twenties, wearing a tan-puppy-toothed cap, took the stool next to me. He clenched a half-chewed, unlit cigar in his teeth. He ordered a beer in what sounded like a British accent.

He took the cigar out of his mouth and glanced to make eye contact.

"Good day, mate."

Lefty looked around me and nodded his head in recognition of the stranger.

"You from England?" I asked as I flipped open the Zippo and offered him a light.

He leaned toward the lighter and drew the flame into the soggy cigar until it was lit. He blew smoke out of the corner of his mouth.

"No. Down under."

Jim placed an ashtray in front of him.

With a confused look, I asked, "Down under?"

He looked straight ahead, worked his cigar, and drank from his beer.

"Australia."

I raised my glass to Jim for a refill.

"What's an Australian doing here in San Francisco?"

"Passing through. I was crabbing up in Alaska and now on my way down to Nicaragua."

Lefty and I shot a look at each other in wonderment. I offered him my hand as Jim placed a fresh tumbler in front of me.

"I'm Tony and this is Lefty."

Lefty reached in front of me, offered his hand, and called out, "Hey Jim, bring another beer for," and looked at the stranger.

"What's your name?"

"Macy, Macy McDonald."

"Bring another beer for our new Aussie friend Macy," Lefty ordered.

"Thanks, mate," as he eyed the fresh beer before him.

"How was the crabbing up in Alaska?" Lefty asked.

"Pretty good, had a bumper year."

"Where do you crab up there?" I asked.

I knew absolutely nothing about crabbing in Alaska.

"We fish out of Dutch Harbor in the Bering Sea."

"Sounds brutal," I continued.

"Can be at times."

"Doesn't it get wicked cold up there?" asked Lefty.

"Colder than a witch's tit, but the money's good for a month's work."

"How did you get into that?" I asked.

"I went up there and asked for a job. They're always short of crew."

"How did you even hear about it?" Lefty butted in.

"A friend and I in Southeast Alaska panned for gold. The crab season opened up, so I decided to try it."

"That's a ballsy move," said Lefty. "Tell me more about gold panning. Did you make any money doing that?"

"We did all right, but it's arduous work with shoveling and sluicing. The mosquitos and no-see-ums are so bad they tear the shit out of you. Not to say nothing about the bears that came into our camp to eat our food stuff."

"BEARS!" Lefty shouted. "I knew bears were up there, but I never knew anyone who encountered one.?"

Macy glanced at Lefty, "Big grizzlies that can tear your face off with one swipe of their claws."

"Wow!" Lefty exclaimed, "Anybody get hurt by bears while you were there?"

"Sure did, mate, three attacks, close to us. One girl attacked while jogging. They only found body parts, strung out along the trail."

"Oh man!" said Lefty. "I can see how you would rather fish than be torn up by a bear."

Lefty caught Jim's attention and made a circle in the air with his forefinger pointed at each of us. Jim nodded and refreshed our drinks.

Macy took a drink and asked, "You know of a good place to eat around here?"

"Of course, we do," I answered. "We know all the places around here. What are you looking for?"

"Not seafood, I've been eating seafood until it's coming out of my ears."

"Some great Italian places, steak houses, Chinese, you name it, this is San Francisco."

"I'd die for a pizza, anything like that close?"

"A good pizza restaurant is down the street. It's close enough you can walk to," I added.

"Hey Tone, let's drink up and take him there. I'm hungry myself. You don't mind if we join you, do you Macy?" Lefty asked.

"Hell no, I'd appreciate it. Good to know blokes who know their way around."

We got off our stools, and Jim came up.

"That'll be seventeen bucks, boys."

Lefty and I reached into our pockets, pulled out ten dollars each, and tossed them on the bar.

"We'll pick up Macy's tab and keep the change, Jim."

"Thanks fellas. See you next time around," Jim answered.

CHAPTER 2

We stood out on the windy street, "We'll go in my car and I'll bring you back." I said.

"I thought you said it was walking distance?" asked Macy.

I pointed to my red Corvette convertible, still new enough to smell the fresh leather seats, "It is, but I don't want to leave my car here with the top down."

"Nice car," said Macy. "But there is only room enough for two."

"No problem, Lefty will ride queer in the middle."

Impressed by my car, Macy asked, "What do you do for a living?"

Lefty and I grinned at each other.

Lefty answered, "We'll tell you later."

Lefty slid into the middle. I started up the Corvette. The engine roared to life, and I gunned it to give Macy a thrill.

Lefty leaned forward next to Macy's ear on the short ride to the pizza joint.

"You said you're headed to Nicaragua. What do you plan to do there?"

"Buy gold on the Rio Coco."

"Rio Coco! What's the Rio Coco?"

"It's the river on the border between Nicaragua and Honduras."

"There's gold there?" Lefty asked excitedly.

"Supposed to be lots of it," Macy answered.

I pulled my red Corvette in front of an old 1920s, two-story green Victorian building. It sat on a corner lot. Tony's Pizza Napolitana, stenciled on the red awning over the sidewalk.

I turned off the engine as Macy looked inside the crowded pizza joint.

"There are some nice-looking Sheilas in there," Macy said.

"Sheilas?" I asked, confused. "What's a Sheila?"

"It's what we call girls down under."

"There are hot chicks that come here. It's a hang- out for them. Did we bring you to the right place?"

"I'm not complaining," Macy answered.

Lefty hesitated and sat back like he was deep in thought.

I stood ready to close the car door.

"Are you coming?" I asked Lefty.

He looked up and slid across the seat.

Several girls checked us out as we entered the pizza joint. We were the center of attention with the red Corvette parked out front.

We took a table next to the window and checked out the girls who checked out the car. In the far corner was a blazing brick oven. There was a slight scent of yeast as the pie maker twirled fresh dough in the air.

A pretty waitress with bright oval jade eyes and a moonbeam smile handed us menus.

"Hi, I'm Tracy. What can I bring you to drink?"

Lefty didn't ask me or Macy when he ordered a pitcher of beer.

We waited for our drinks while Macy looked at the menu. "What do you suggest?"

"We always order a large with everything on it," Lefty answered

"Sounds good to me," said Macy and closed the menu. "You guys never told me what you do for work?"

The waitress brought the pitcher of beer and three glasses.

"Have you figured out what you want to order?" she asked as she poured beer into the glasses.

Lefty looked at her.

"We'll take a large with everything on it."

Before the waitress could write anything down, Macy butted in.

"We better make that two. I'm famished and the pizza is on me."

The waitress heard Macy's accent and looked at him. "Oh, I love your accent! Are you from England?"

We looked at each other and smiled as Macy looked up at her.

"No, Sweetheart, Australia."

"I love it!" she squealed. "Two large with everything, coming right up."

She returned to the kitchen. She stopped another waitress, said something in her ear, and then nodded toward our table. The other girl looked our way and looked back at the waitress as they giggled.

As we drank our beer, Macy tried again, "What kind of work are you two in?"

"We run an escort business," I answered, looking at the girls outside, who were also looking at my car.

Macy sat down his beer on the table in a semi-state of shock.

"What kind of escort business?"

"The kind that takes out lonely women, treats them nice and gets paid for it," jumped in Lefty.

Macy looked staggered as if trying to gather his thoughts on what he had heard. Lefty and I continued to drink as if what we were doing was perfectly normal.

"I wouldn't mind getting laid while I'm here. Do you have any phone numbers?" Macy asked.

"Can't give them to you," I answered.

"Why not?" Macy pressured.

"It would be bad for business," I countered.

Macy didn't give up, "Bad for business. What do you mean bad for business?"

Lefty said, "Look, Macy, you're a cool guy and we like you. It's nothing personal, but we can't give out phone numbers. What we do is strictly confidential and if our clients got wind that we passed out phone numbers we'd be out of business in no time."

Macy backed off when the waitress brought the pizzas.

She placed the pizzas on the table and spent an inordinate amount of time making sure Macy was satisfied. Her interest in him was obvious. She hesitated and watched Macy take his first bite of pizza.

"If you need anything else, let me know," looking directly at Macy.

As this drama unfolded, Lefty said, "Besides, with your cute little down under accent, I don't think you'll have a problem getting laid."

We wolfed down the pizza and finished the beer.

I announced, "I have to get going. I have a work date tonight."

Macy waved to the waitress to bring the tab. She started coming, turned around, and returned to the cash register to write something down. She laid the check on the table, and Macy looked at the amount. He reached into his back pocket, took out cash, and handed it to the waitress.

"Keep the change," he said.

She thanked him and slid a note under his plate. It was easy for Lefty and me to notice. She cleared the pitcher and glasses and left.

Macy picked up the note and glanced at it.

"What does it say?" Lefty begged.

He turned it so we could read.

I'm off at eight, with her phone number underneath, signed, Tracy.

We got up to leave when Lefty rubbed Macy's head, "There you go Aussie wonder. Looks like you scored!"

Macy looked at him with a sheepish grin.

Outside, Lefty asked Macy, "Where are you staying?"

"At the Thunderbird on Lombard Street."

"I'll take you there," Lefty offered. He wanted to grill him on this Nicaraguan gold on the way.

We stood on the sidewalk and shook hands. Macy thanked us for our help. I drove off and thought that was the last I'd see of Macy.

CHAPTER 3

My white three-bedroom bungalow overlooked the Great Highway to Ocean Beach and the Pacific. The large picture window faced the ocean to watch the moods of the Pacific Ocean while I entertained my clients with my home-cooked cuisine.

I cleaned up from a date the night before when the phone rang.

I figured it was Lefty, "Yeah man, what's up?"

"What did you think of that Australian guy?" Lefty asked without an introduction.

"Seemed like a pretty cool guy. He sure gets around. What did you think about him?" I asked.

"He is an interesting guy. After I took him back to his hotel, I spent time together with him for a while and we talked about this gold thing."

"Seems like you're interested in what he had to say."

"That's not the half of it. You know, before he went to Alaska, he mined gold in Costa Rica?"

"That's interesting. How did that happen?"

"He collaborated with this American guy and made a ton of money."

"Did he call up that girl from the pizza joint?"

"I don't know. He said he was going to, but I left before he did."

Lefty laughed and continued, "He is supposed to meet that American guy in Nicaragua, and they're going up the Rio Coco together and look for gold. What do you think about getting involved?"

"Not much. I've been down in that part of the world and it's not safe. Besides, I got a good thing going here."

"I know you do, but it would be an adventure and we might strike it rich."

"I have all the money I need. Didn't you hear the part where he almost got attacked by grizzlies? He walks a tight rope. It sounds like more than I want to manage right now."

"Look Tony, you're flush with money and life is going your way. But think about me. I don't have what you have. All I have is this crazy chick who wants me to dress up as a girl and go shopping. I was hoping you'd be up for this."

"Jeez Lefty, I don't know what to say. Why don't you go without me? Macy will show you around."

"I haven't asked him about going along. Besides, I wouldn't go without you. I didn't want to say anything until I talked to you."

"You're putting me on the spot. I really don't know what to say."

I sensed I took the wind out of his sails and felt terrible for him. We'd been friends since elementary school and grew up together. I waited for his reply.

He sounded disappointed and sighed, "All right, if that's the way you feel."

Feeling bad, I tried to humor him.

"How long is he going to be in town?"

He jumped on it.

"Three or four days, I got his room number and gave him my phone number."

"I'll tell you what. I'm not going to promise you anything, but if you can pull it together, we can see him again and find out about the details. But don't get your hopes up, it sounds shaky to me."

"I know no promises. I get it, but I can't see where it'd hurt to talk to him."

"Get back to me when you put something together. I'm not doing much for the next couple of days, so we have time to check it out."

"Great, man. I will. Thanks, ol' buddy."

Two hours later, Lefty called me back. "Hey Tone! I was going to call Macy when he called me. The guy he was to meet in Nicaragua, his wife is filing for divorce, and he can't meet up with him."

"That sounds fishy to me."

"Might be, but he needs to hang around for a few more days and wants to know if there was a cheaper place to stay."

"Does that mean, could he stay with one of us?"

"He implied that, yes."

"This is getting weirder by the moment. We don't know the guy, and now he wants to stay with one of us. If he made so much money in Alaska, why is looking for cheap living arrangements? What did you tell him?"

"I'd have to talk to you first."

"Thanks for getting me tangled up in this. You know how I feel about it."

"But this could be legit. I hate to shine him on. We should at least hear what he has to say."

"Man, Lefty! I don't know."

"What say we hear him out? Can't hurt anything. Besides, you want to know if he got laid by that girl at the pizza joint."

After a pause, "I guess it can't hurt. Where do you want to meet?"

"I already worked that out."

"Damn, Lefty, nothing like assuming shit."

"Don't have a shit fit. I told him I didn't know if you were available."

"Thanks for being so considerate."

"Come on, Tone. Don't get weird on me. If you don't want to meet the guy, say so."

Another pause as I tried to hold back my temper, "Okay. Where are we going to meet?"

"I told him if you agreed, and I did say if you agreed, I'd pick him up and meet you back at Tony Nik's at six-thirty."

"All right, all right… I'll be there, but don't get your hopes up."

"Don't worry, I'm cool with it."

"Ah bullshit!" I shouted as I slammed down the phone.

CHAPTER 4

Streetlights lit the road in front of Tony Nik's. Lefty's car was parked out front. The only available parking spot for me was a block down the street.

I was tight-jawed. At least the son of a bitch could have left that spot open for me. I wasn't in a good mood.

Lefty wasn't in the darkened bar. I figured they must be in the lounge.

The softly lit room meant for romantic interludes felt out of place for discussing gold hunting in Nicaragua. Lefty and Macy nursed their beers in the back corner. Locked in a conversation, they didn't notice me until I stood at the table and waited for a greeting.

"Hey Tone, pull up a chair," offered Lefty.

Another strike against Lefty was when I had to get a chair from another table and drag it over.

Macy offered his hand. "Hi, mate."

I nodded and looked at Macy when Jim, the bartender, produced a Jack Daniels on the rocks and placed it on the table.

Lefty tried to break the ice when he noticed the coolness of my attitude by blurting out a nervous announcement, "He scored!"

I looked at Lefty expressionless and sipped my bourbon.

"What do you mean?"

"He scored! The girl from the pizza place!"

"Oh yeah?" I answered as I glanced at Macy.

"He did. Don't you want to hear about it?"

Unenthusiastically, I answered, "Sure,"

Lefty struggled to liven things up. "He called her at eight and she came to his hotel. They didn't even go anywhere. Inside of twenty minutes they were humping like a couple rabbits, right on the bed. What do you think of our Aussie wonder?"

Macy looked uncomfortable and held his beer with both hands. It was apparent that something was going on between Lefty and me.

I took a big swig of Jack Daniel's to calm down and realized with my aggravation with Lefty, I was being rude to Macy.

"How was it?" I asked Macy, as I tried to sound genuinely interested.

"Pretty good."

"How did you leave it?" Lefty pressured. "You going to see her again?"

"I got her number," Macy answered.

Lefty tried to move the conversation along.

"I don't know much about Australia. What goes down there?"

"About the same as goes on here."

"What kind of work did you do down there?"

"I worked in the mines with my father until I got into boxing."

When he mentioned boxing, my interest heightened. I checked out Macy's physique: we were about the same size and build, and even our complexion was the same. The difference was in our facial features; Macy's nose bent crooked and took sharp jabs.

"Boxing!" Lefty exclaimed. "Now we're talking. I'm a boxing fanatic. What weight class were you in?"

I sipped my drink and let Lefty keep the conversation going, but I began to take an interest in this man from "down under," myself.

"Lightweight," Macy answered.

"Lightweight!" Lefty prodded. "How did you get into boxing?"

"I wanted to get out of the mines, so when a boxing troop came to town and they needed a lightweight fighter, I joined up."

"What's a boxing troop?" asked Lefty.

"Tent boxing, mate. We went to outback towns and set up a tent then challenged the local toughs to a fight."

"What I want to know is how you went from boxing to mining gold?"

"I traveled to Costa Rica and was drinking at this bar where I met an American gold miner out on the Pacific Coast. After I heard his story, I asked if he needed help. He invited me out to have a look, so I went and started shoveling."

"Did he pay you?" Lefty questioned.

"No, mate, I got a percentage of the take."

"You made money?"

"I did, but it's a hard life."

Jim brought another round of drinks with a bowl of peanuts. I didn't say anything, not swayed by the romance, as Lefty was.

I pictured the hard life Macy talked about and thought back to the mosquitos and grizzlies, which dampened my enthusiasm. Macy's stories kept me hanging on, but you could count me out unless he produced groundbreaking revelations.

Lefty wanted to hear more.

"What's with this Nicaraguan gold, how did that come about?" asked Lefty.

"It's easier to buy gold cheap upriver and sell it dear, than break your back mining it, mate. When my friend found out there was cheap gold on the Rio Coco, he asked me if I wanted to go along."

Lefty quieted down momentarily, then took a drink from his beer and asked.

"Why Nicaragua?"

"There are no rules down there, which lowers the price and adds to the profit."

"Doesn't it add to the risk?" I asked.

"The greater the risk, the greater the reward," answered Macy

"Now that your friend backed out, what do you plan to do?" asked Lefty.

"I have to hang around here until he contacts a man in Nicaragua. It will take time to work things out."

"You'd go on your own?" Lefty curiously asked.

"I went to Costa Rica, Alaska and fishing on my own. You talk to people and pieces come together. So far it's worked for me."

"You're a ballsy guy, to say the least," answered Lefty.

Macy tilted his head and took a drink of his beer.

"You mentioned a cheaper place to stay while you waited?" asked Lefty.

"I don't mean to be a burden, but it would be nice. I was going to leave the day after tomorrow, but with what happened, I have to wait for a week or so. If there is something available?"

Lefty looked at me, pleading. After I heard Macy's story, I wasn't sure how I felt.

Macy noticed this. "I need to take a piss fellas. Where's the head?" he asked.

"Around the corner, to the left," Lefty pointed.

With Macy gone, Lefty asked.

"What do you think?"

"I think he's an interesting guy."

"I know that, but what about giving him a place to stay?"

"If you're so excited about this, let him stay at your place," I answered shortly.

"He could stay at my place, but I have a one-bedroom flat, you have a three-bedroom house on the beach."

"You know you're starting to piss me off."

"Don't get pissed off. It's only for a couple of days, what's the big deal? Can't we help the guy out?"

Macy came back before we reached an agreement. He took a drink of his beer as Lefty announced, "You can stay at Tony's."

I felt betrayed. I held my tongue and thought maybe I could protect Lefty if I knew Macy better. Besides, I started to like the guy.

"That's okay with you, mate?"

After a short pause, Lefty held his breath.

"You can stay at my place. How long do you need?" I answered.

Lefty sighed in relief as Macy answered, "It won't be long. As soon as I receive a telegram from my friend in Costa Rica telling me he has plans to go with the newspaperman to get me to Rio Coca, then I'll be off. I do need to know where the closest telegraph office is here."

I turned the tables on Lefty. "Don't worry about that, Lefty will show you around, won't you Lefty?"

He jerked his head up. "Sure, I have time, no problem, let me know what you need."

Jim came up to see how our drinks were holding out. "Another round, boys?"

"I'm hungry," answered Lefty. "What say I take you guys out and get a steak somewhere?"

I was shocked Lefty would make such an offer, "Where do you want to go?" I asked

"Let's go to the Cliff House. It's down by your place."

I knew Lefty caught gold fever. His exuberance would cost me money down the line to keep him out of trouble.

"I'll meet you there," I answered. Macy picked up the tab.

CHAPTER 5

At the parking lot on Lobos Point, overlooking the ruins of Sutro Baths, we took a moment to explain to Macy the history of Adolph Sutro before we entered the aging two-story Cliff House restaurant. The spacious dining room gave us a panoramic view of Seal Rock and the Pacific Ocean, but one couldn't miss the odor of years gone by. We sat at the same table where Teddy Roosevelt sat decades before.

The server passed out the menus. "What can I get you to drink, gentlemen?"

Lefty looked at his menu, "Double Seagram's. Straight up."

I winced. Lefty didn't do well with hard liquor.

"Celebrating?" I asked.

Lefty smiled.

"This is a nice place," stated Macy.

"Everybody who comes through here should experience the Cliff House. Don't you think, Tone?"

"It's a popular place," I answered, with a lingering stare to let Lefty know I knew what he was up to.

Lefty focused his conversation on Macy's boxing exploits.

Macy explained that although he wasn't an active boxer anymore, he stayed in shape and sometimes sparred against someone.

Seagram's 7 soon took its effect. In his semi-drunken state, Lefty told Macy that he sometimes spent time at the Third Street Boxing Gym and said he could take him down there.

Before the night was over, after his third Seagram's, Lefty challenged Macy to a round. Lefty needed to be in better shape, and his boxing skills were limited. Macy tried to give Lefty an out by politely turning him down. Still, Lefty vehemently insisted until Macy accepted the challenge. I wasn't going to miss this mismatch for the world.

After we finished our meals, the waitress laid the bill on the table as Macy and I left. Lefty looked at the bill and saw that the total was well over the twenty dollars he had in his pocket.

I squinted my eyes at him. I knew I was going to be on the hook for this meal.

He rushed to me while I opened the door to let Macy out, "Hey Tone, can I see you for a second?"

With Macy on the porch, I knew what was coming. "Yeah, man. What's up?"

"Could you help me out here?" Lefty asked. "I don't have the money to cover the bill."

I looked at him and rolled my eyes. "You know when you ask someone out to dinner you're supposed to pay for it."

"I know. I wasn't thinking."

I took the bill from Lefty's outstretched hand and huffed over to the cashier.

CHAPTER 6

I rked at Lefty when I got out of bed, I noticed Macy's room door open. He was gone. He had made the bed, and his clothes were stacked neatly in his suitcase. This guy is no flake; he actually made his bed! I prepared a pot of coffee.

I wondered where Macy was and scanned the area on the front porch. A slight mist fell from the low overcast skies as a scent of rotting seaweed came up from the sandy beach. Along the surf line, a lone figure jogged down the beach, leaving indented tracks in the hard-packed sand.

I looked at my watch. Eight o'clock. Lefty would pick up Macy and take him to the gym at ten. I grabbed my first cup of coffee and went out on the porch, where I found Macy in shorts and a tee shirt.

Macy leaned over the railing and clapped his shoes together to knock off the loose sand.

"Coffee's on," I shouted.

"Thanks, mate. Mind if I leave me shoes on the porch to dry? They got a wee bit wet."

"By all means, let's go inside and get you a cup."

We sipped our coffee, and Macy said, "I appreciate you letting me stay here."

"No problem, I live here alone, so there's enough room. We have a big match today."

"I guess so."

"Hope you take it easy on Lefty. He can get a bit blustery after a couple of drinks," as I topped off the cups.

"Don't we all." Macy laughed.

I met Lefty and Macy at the gym and looked at Lefty. "You up for this, Marciano?"

"Hell, yes, I'm up for it. Did you think I'd back out like a wuss?"

I laughed and looked at Macy. "You better be careful. You got a real gorilla here."

Lefty blurted, "You've never been in the ring with anybody. Besides, I'm defending our nation against these Australian hordes trying to take our chicks."

We laughed as we entered the gym. Lefty looked over at the front counter where Max the manager sat back on a black roller chair and twisted the hairs of his gray Manchurian mustache.

"How's it going, Max?"

"Going good, Lefty. Who you got with you?"

"Macy is a professional boxer who fought in Australia, and we wanted to show him the gym and do a little sparring. I don't see anybody in the ring. Can we take it for half an hour?"

"I don't see a problem. You're going to need gloves and headgear."

Max took two sets of sixteen-ounce gloves, which hung on the wall, and placed them on the counter. He looked at Lefty and Macy for a second as he sized them up and pulled out headgear.

Lefty laid a ten-spot on the counter, and they headed for the locker room. Unable to ignore the sweaty body odor, I looked around. The ring was in the middle of the gym. On the far side were heavy bags, speed balls, and an uppercut bag that hung from the ceiling. Hand wraps and jump ropes strung on nails haphazardly banged into the wall amongst the colorful posters of fights long past.

Lefty and Macy came out of the locker room wearing shorts, their hands wrapped. They jumped rope to warm up. Macy knew what he was doing, and I wondered again if Lefty had made the right decision to spar. He was really out of shape.

Lefty watched Macy out of the corner of his eye. Macy was a joy to watch. He barely lifted his feet as he crossed the rope before him. Lefty finished skipping rope and had Max lace on his gloves. Macy worked the speedball before asking me over to help with his gloves.

Macy climbed through the ropes. In the ring, he danced lightly and threw punches at shadows.

"Ready, mate?" Macy asked and gave Lefty a wink. Lefty slowly entered the ring. I moved to the apron and thought this would be a massacre. They began to fight.

Macy threw the first jab and caught Lefty on the chin. Lefty tried to counter and missed as Macy bobbed his head to the left. He tried again, caught Macy on the shoulder, and backed away. Macy moved in and threw a right. Lefty saw it coming and covered his face with his gloves to deflect the impact. He countered with a body punch that landed in Macy's ribs. They both backed away and shuffled their feet.

Macy connected with a jab, then dropped his shoulder before he followed it with an uppercut, which caught Lefty on the point of the chin. The ropes saved him from going down.

Macy reached out to help steady him. "You all right, mate?"

"A lucky shot. Come on, put 'em up. Let's go."

They started to move around again. It looked like Macy had backed off, which made Lefty angry. He came in swinging, and Macy ducked and weaved, which caused Lefty to miss, which made him madder.

Macy charged in and caught Lefty with a right cross that sent him to the mat. I wanted to stop the fight before Lefty lost more composure and made a complete fool of himself.

Lefty jumped up from the mat and swung wildly. Macy covered up with his gloves, his elbows tucked into his side to protect himself from the glancing body shots. He leaned against the ropes and took everything Lefty had to offer. The punches did no harm.

Lefty punched himself out; sweat flowed down his face and dripped off the tip of his nose. He hunched forward, his arms hung down, as he panted for breath.

Macy dropped the gloves and looked at the worn-out Lefty, "Good fight, mate. What say we get a beer?"

Lefty stared at him as he gasped for air, "Sure."

Back at Tony Nik's was a bonding moment for us as we laughed and teased each other after the fight. Lefty had hung in there and finished the fight, knowing he was the lesser man.

I had a new appreciation for Macy. He could have easily knocked Lefty out, but remained in control, proving the man he was. I was surprised at myself when, suddenly, the search for gold in Nicaragua didn't seem so far-fetched.

"Nicaragua. Have you spent time there?" I asked.

Lefty looked at me as he heard the word Nicaragua, then looked at Macy to await his answer.

"I took a quick trip to Managua while in Costa Rica," Macy said.

"You'd be going in cold, not knowing much?"

"Not totally. An American guy in Managua who runs an English-speaking newspaper has been down there for years. He's the guy we're trying to locate. He likes good local stories for his paper and could point us in the right direction."

Lefty couldn't hold back any longer, "What if someone wanted to go along? Someone like me and Tony."

I broke in. "Let's say like Lefty."

Lefty looked at me, disappointed.

"I don't know, mate. I'd have to think it over. It wasn't in my plans. I really don't want to commit to anything right now. Still waiting on that telegram."

Despite my clear reservations, l wanted to know how it worked.

"How much do you invest when you get down there?" I continued. "Would two grand be a good number?"

"Two grand? That's a suitable number," Macy answered.

"Can you double your money?"

"At least," Macy answered, looking at me and sipping his beer.

Chapter 7

The next couple of days were uneventful. Lefty used the time to show Macy around the Bay Area and checked the Western Union office twice daily for telegrams.

That gave me time to reflect. Still hesitant, I knew Lefty would be all in if Macy gave the go-ahead. I checked my bank account and called the airline to see what it cost to fly down there. I wasn't going to let Lefty go on his own. I was in a holding mode. I was curious to see what transpired from the Western Union office.

I'd started cooking up lemon garlic chicken when they burst into the house after a trip to Western Union.

"We got it!" cried Lefty, waving the telegram.

"What does it say?" I asked as I added croutons to the salad.

Lefty looked at Macy. "Do you mind reading it?"

Macy sat down:

> *Contacted John Weismann in Managua—stop—Willing to help you get to Rio Coca—stop—Call him before you comes—stop—Good luck—stop.*

"That's welcome news," I answered as I checked the chicken in the oven. "So, what are your plans?"

"If I can use your phone, I'll call him tomorrow. After I talk with him, I'll arrange a flight and clear out."

"For your information, I called the airport this morning. There's an afternoon flight at two for Mexico City with connections to Managua on

Pan Am, arriving at nine in the morning."

With a confused look, Lefty asked me, "Why did you check the flights?"

"Curious, Lefty, just curious."

I took out the chicken and placed it on the table, "Let's eat."

Lefty took a bite and said, "Hey Tone, Macy and I were talking. Macy says he wouldn't mind if we came along with him."

"Is that right, Macy?" I asked.

"I wouldn't mind company for the ride. Let's see what unfolds."

"Hmm," I answered. "Lefty, How much money do you have to take down?"

"I thought if you helped me with the fare, I could put together a thousand."

"What would you do if you lost it all?"

"I have that plump girl with the blue lipstick."

CHAPTER 8

Pan Am flight 64 touched down at the Las Mercedes Airport in Managua right on time. The ground crew rolled up the stairway to the plane. The flight attendant opened the door, and a rush of hot, humid air flooded the plane.

We started down the stairway, and Lefty noted, "Sure is hot down here."

In the terminal were three Customs desks with passengers lined up to show passports and visas.

"They have good cigars down here," Macy remarked

"Where do you get them?" Lefty asked.

"There is a small kiosk once we get through here. You can buy a pack of ten for five dollars."

Macy's friend in Costa Rica arranged for us to meet John Weismann in the lobby of the Gran Hotel in downtown Managua. John arranged transportation to Puerto Cabezas on the Atlantic coast.

Out of the airport, a cigar hung from Lefty's mouth. "One of you guys have a light?" Lefty asked.

I lit his cigar with my Zippo. "Shit, Lefty, you don't have a match?"

"No, I don't have a match. What's your problem?"

Macy reached into his pocket and took out a book of matches. "Here, mate, keep these."

"Thanks, at least I know who my friends are," Lefty replied as he glared at me.

Taxis lined up on the curb. We puffed on our stogies as our shirts soaked with dripping sweat. A taxi driver leaned on the door and called out, "Taxi?"

With backpacks slung over our shoulders, we crammed into the taxi, filled with cigar smoke.

The driver started the engine. "Where to?" he asked.

I was pleasantly surprised that the driver spoke English. That would make things much easier.

"The Gran Hotel," Macy answered.

Lefty puffed on his cigar and commented, "These are pretty damned good. What do they call these down here?"

"El Puro, Mate. If you like cigars, you've come to the right place."

On the way to the hotel, we stared in awe at the strangeness of the city. Macy had seen it before, but it was a new experience for Lefty and me.

Lefty looked out the window, "Hey look at that. It's a live volcano. Look at the steam coming out of the top."

"That's Masaya. I went to the top last time I was here."

Macy looked at me. "You haven't said much. Are you all right?"

"I'm worried about the cash we have on us. I'll perk up when I get a drink in me." I took another long pull on my cigar.

In front of the hotel, we gazed up at the large columns across the front. The street was packed with cars and shoppers. Modern shops with neon signs hung over the sidewalk.

The hotel door attendant opened the glass door. "Buenas tardes," he greeted.

"Ahh, air conditioning," Lefty shouted.

Two men sat in the lobby on wicker chairs next to glass-top tables. One overweight man with red hair and a ginger complexion wore a white duck suit with no tie. The other, a bearded man, wore an epauletted tan L.L.Bean poplin shirt with sleeves rolled up with an olive drab journalist's vest. He took notes on a thin tablet as they talked.

We stood at the check-in desk when the man in the white suit got up and came our way.

"Hello, gentlemen. Is one of you Macy McDonald?"

"I am. John Weismann, I assume."

"Yes." He reached out his hand. "Nice to meet you. Who are these other gentlemen with you?"

"This is Tony Taylor and Lefty Jackson." We shook hands.

"Welcome to Nicaragua. Once you check in, come over and join us. Can I order you a drink?"

"Very kind of you, mate. I'll take a Victoria beer."

"Good enough for me," said Lefty.

"I hear the rum is good down here?" I asked.

"It is," answered John. "Flor de Cana, the flower of the cane. Would you like rum and Coke?"

"Be great, thanks," I answered.

Our drinks were on the table when we joined them. John and the other man stood up.

"Let me introduce you to Hal Moore," said John. "Hal is a reporter with the Reuters News Agency." After formal greetings, he added, "Hal is investigating a story on the lobster divers in the Miskito Keys."

"The Miskito Keys?" I asked.

"The Miskito Keys are a group of coral islands off the Atlantic Coast." John looked at Hal. "Hal can explain the situation better than I can."

In a deep voice, Hal replied, "Sure. From what I understand, you're going out to the Caribbean coast?"

"That's right," Macy answered, not ready to give up the reason.

"It's a different world out there. The Atlantic side is autonomous. It used to be thriving while the Standard Fruit Company had operations there, but with Sandino's revolution it stagnated. The Miskito, Sumo, and Rama Indians who live there have always been independent. They got angry when the fruit company brought in Jamaicans to work their plantations and it caused problems."

"What do the Indians do for work?" I asked.

"They are hunter-gatherers. Fishing mostly, they net for shrimp and snook off the beach for cash and sell to a local Creole man named George Morgan. Morgan set up ice and seafood processing plants up and down the coast. They say he's related to Henry Morgan, the English pirate. They carve dugout canoes which they paddle out about a mile or so and fish to feed their families. The more industrious ones make charcoal, plant cassava and corn out in the jungle."

"I have two questions," asked Lefty. "What's a snook and what's a Creole?"

"Snook is a thick, flaky, white meat fish. Looks like a Northern Pike, with an international market. Creoles are Caribbean Black people often mixed with local Indians."

I worried about my limited Spanish. "Do they speak Spanish out there?"

"Not much, the women mostly speak Miskito, but what they call the King's English is widely spoken."

"That's good news," I answered.

"Tell them about the divers," John interrupted.

"Of course. Morgan set up the Miskitos with dive tanks and compressors. He owns a couple of boats and sends them out to the keys to dive for spiny lobster. They bring a big return, both for the locals and export."

"It's the problem I want you to explain to them, the reason you're here," John insisted.

"I'm getting to that. How are we set for drinks? Looks like you're ready for more."

"I am," I answered. "I'll get this round."

"Does this place serve food? I'm starving?" Lefty barked.

"They have great hamburgers," John informed him.

"Hamburgers!" answered Lefty. "Down here? French fries come with it?"

We ordered hamburgers from the waiter as John pushed again, "Okay, Hal, tell them the rest."

"Right. The problem is they strap air tanks on the divers and send them down without any training."

"That is a problem. They get the bends?" Macy remarked.

"They do. If it doesn't kill them, when you go to the villages, you'll see them walking around on crutches, shitting and pissing over themselves."

"What are they doing about it?" I asked.

"Right now, nothing. Part of the problem is the Miskito themselves. They're a macho group. People have gone out to try and instruct them in the proper way to dive, but they don't pay any attention; they think they know better."

"That's fucked up!" Lefty exclaimed as the waiter brought the hamburgers.

John said, "Tell them what you're doing about it, Hal."

"It's an exceptional story and opportunity for photos. I was invited by a Peace Corp doctor who's trying to raise money for a decompression chamber. She figures if we make people aware of the problem, it will be easier to raise money to buy the chamber."

"She! That's interesting, mate. How come she picked you?"

"Let me answer that for you, Hal," John said. "Hal is an award-winning journalist. He's worked in Latin America for years. With his world of knowledge, he's savvy about what is happening south of the border. You're lucky to have him in your midst. I haven't said much to him about what you're up to, but if you have any questions, it would be in your interests to ask him."

Macy hesitated for a moment, then looked at Hal. "We're going up the Rio Coco to buy gold."

"Rio Coco, huh. How much do you know about it?"

"Not much. I mined gold in Costa Rica for a while with a bloke, and he told me about it. He said the Indians have placer mines on the river. They get good gold and sell it at a reasonable price."

"Do you have buyers?" Hal asked. "It's none of my business, but there's a reason I'm asking."

Macy nodded. "I have buyers."

I was nervous about Macy being so coy. Hal was a straight shooter, and I wanted to gain as much as possible. Lefty asked for another beer.

Hal continued, "There is a mining company out of Canada running a big operation north of Bonanza."

"Where is Bonanza?" Macy asked.

"Twenty-five miles northwest of Rosita on Route 218."

John said, "You take 218 out to Puerto Cabezas, Rosita is halfway."

"How far is that from Rio Coco? Can we get to Rio Coco from there?" Macy asked.

"No." Hal shook his head. "It's about sixty miles through thick jungle. There are old mule trails used by the Indians, but you'd never get out alive."

"Why is that?" I nervously asked.

"You'd get lost and starve to death. The mining company is having trouble with lefties who are trying to unionize the workers. It's not a safe place to go right now."

"So how can we get there?"

"The only way in is on Route 218. John has arranged transportation for you."

"A trucker runs cargo out to Puerto Cabezas. He's a good guy and knows his way around," John added. "In Puerto, I've arranged for you to meet an American friend, Brodie West. He'll get you out to Waspam on the Rio Coco, and from there, you charter a boat up to Santa Rita."

"How long does this take?" I asked.

"The road trip takes two days. "You'll stay overnight in Rosita unless Julio wants to drive at night, which I don't recommend," John continued.

"Julio is the driver?" Macy asked.

"That's right. At Waspam the boat trip up the river takes two days as well."

"Where do we stay on the river?" I asked.

Hal shrugged. "The boat handler works that out. They do it all the time."

"What's with Santa Rita?" Macy asked.

"That's where the gold country starts with placer mining," answered John.

"Brodie West, what's his deal?" I asked.

"Brodie West is a legend," Hal explained. "He was in the heaviest fighting with the Marines in Korea. He showed up one day building boats for the local fishermen. He has a hot, deaf, and mute Creole girlfriend named Ona."

Lefty feeling his alcohol said, "Damn man, how do they communicate?"

"They have their ways," answered Hal. "They know what each other's thinking."

"I know what I'd be thinking." Lefty laughed.

"Why are you so concerned about the gold buyers?" I asked Hal.

"The Hondurans are trying to control the gold prices. They're trying to control the whole river, which upset the Nicaraguans. They almost went to war over who owned Edinburgh Reef and the fishing rights there. If you sell gold to the Hondurans, they'll rip you off, if they don't blow your brains out and take it."

"Jesus!" I said under my breath. "Sounds like coming down here was a big mistake."

"It can be if you don't know your way around."

"Is there any money to be made?" Lefty blurted out.

"You can make money, but you have to know what you're doing."

Macy asked, "What's our way around?"

"Brodie West," Hal answered.

"How can we trust him? Why would he want to help us?" Macy questioned.

"He's a friend of ours, and we look out for each other. If John asks Brodie to help you, he won't let you down."

Macy looked at John, "What's in it for you?"

"I'm a newspaper man looking for interesting stories. This could turn out to be an interesting story."

"Even if it goes south?" I asked.

"Let's not look at it that way," John answered. "We'll believe you go out there, have a great adventure and make money."

"Shit!" I responded.

I was not keen on the idea from the get-go, and from what I'd heard, I was less keen. I came to keep Lefty out of trouble, but with Lefty drinking his cares away, I couldn't help but think what a dumb ass, oblivious to what he got us into.

While we talked, an attractive girl, about five foot four with short brown hair came to the table. Her small breasts with hard nipples were outlined under a light gray tank top. Her facial features had a striking resemblance to Ingrid Bergman.

She ignored us and went directly to John. "I hear you have a truck heading to Puerto Cabezas in a couple of days?"

"That's right, Julio should be here any time. After he gathers another load he's heading back out."

"Could you tell him I need a ride?"

"I'll tell him. You going to be at the compound?"

"If I'm not, leave a message, and I'll get back to you."

She turned and looked at Hal. "Great article you put together."

"No problem," Hal responded.

Ignoring the rest of us, she turned and left.

"Who was that?" Lefty asked as his eyes followed her out.

"That was Ally Short, the Peace Corps girl we talked about," John answered.

"Pretty little thing," Lefty commented.

"Don't let that fool you. She is a woman on a mission and can be hell on wheels," said John.

"Hell on wheels you say?"

"That's right," said Hal. "You mess with her and you'll live to regret it."

"You won't mind having her company on your way out to Puerto Cabezas, will you?" John asked.

"Hell no!" Lefty answered.

I wasn't so sure. The situation was getting complicated. The Honduran buyers and the upheaval at the gold mining operation didn't calm my nerves. Ally joining our troop was a dynamic for which I wasn't prepared. She was easy to look at, but I could tell she was a tough operator. With Lefty's hormonal tendencies, he couldn't help but make a fool of himself.

We finished our meal and conversation, and John asked, "What are your plans for this evening?"

"We have no plans. What do you suggest?" Macy answered.

"Are you up for a little night life?"

Lefty, with a stupid grin on his face, looked at Macy and me, "I think we can manage that."

"I'll come by at seven and take you to a place I think you'll enjoy."

CHAPTER 9

John drove up to the hotel in his black 1964 Impala.

"What's this place you're taking us to?" asked Lefty.

"Todo Vale."

"Todo Vale?" Lefty questioned. "What's that mean?"

"Anything goes."

"Anything goes! Does it mean what it says?" asked Macy.

"Pretty much. It's a bar, restaurant, strip joint and whorehouse rolled into one."

"Is the food any good?" I laughed.

"I rate it high on my list. I must warn you. You can spend a lot of money in no time if you start buying girls drinks. I suggest you hold off until after we eat. They charge three to four times more for a drink if you buy for the girl. And it's lemon juice, anyway."

We entered Todo Vale while a naked, dark-skinned woman was on stage in front of a thick maroon velvet curtain. She sat on a chair. Her jet-black hair hung down below her buttocks. She slowly spread and closed her legs, leaving nothing to the imagination. She cupped and squeezed her breasts with a seductive look.

Behind dark gray tables, red cushioned booths lined the black walls, where scantily dressed girls lounged about. A mirrored globe reflected bits of light on the wall. The middle of the room had three sets of leather couches that faced each other, with a short table in between. Samba music played in the background.

We were watching the stage when a topless girl came up to John and gave him a hug. He had been here before. She led us to a set of couches in the center of the room. The topless girl sat on John's lap and asked what we wanted to drink.

"This is quite a place you brought us to, John," said Macy. "You come here a lot?"

"The girls are friendly and I've gotten to know them. I suggest the churrasco strip steak," he said. "But if you like shrimp, you're in for a treat."

Lefty watched the girl on stage. "I'd like that little dish up there."

"Hey Lefty, you came here to make money, not spend it," I said.

Lefty looked at John. "What's the service charge here?"

"Like I said, you can spend a lot of money."

A couple of girls came our way. John looked at them and wagged his index finger no. They turned around and went back to where they were.

The topless girl came with the drinks, and we ordered our meals. John leaned toward Macy. "Julio, the driver, is in town, I'm going to meet with him tomorrow. Will you be around?"

"We don't have any set plans. I thought of taking my mates up to the Itapúa volcano, but what time are you going to meet with him?"

"He brought in produce that he's going to unload tomorrow at the market. I'm going to meet him there around nine. It might be good if you came along."

"Is Ally going to be with you?" I asked.

"She will."

"Shit!" Lefty shouted. "I wanted to see the volcano."

I was anxious to get moving. "We're coming back through here on our way out, and you'll have a pocket full of gold. You can fuck these whores and see the volcano on your own dime."

Lefty glared at me and settled into his steak, the most expensive order on the menu.

Halfway through his meal, he looked up at me. "Fuck you, Tony!"

"Fuck you," I shot back.

"You've been a dickhead ever since we got here."

"I've been a dickhead!" I answered as I put down my knife and fork. "Does the fact that I'm footing your bill bother you?"

"Hell no, it doesn't bother me. I told you I'd pay you back."

"Pay me back! With what?"

"With the gold we're going to get, asshole."

"Now I'm an asshole. Weren't you listening to what Hal said? The way I figure it, it will be unsure if we can get out of here unscathed. The only reason I came along was to try keep you out of trouble."

"I can take care of myself. Why don't you back off!"

Macy jumped in to calm things down. "Come on fellas, this isn't the place to discuss this. Let's wait until we get back to the hotel. Think of John here, he doesn't need to hear this."

John glanced up from his plate. "Doesn't bother me. It'll make great copy."

"AH SHIT!" Lefty glared and concentrated on his steak..

I returned to my steak with nothing resolved.

After the meal, John announced, "I've got to leave. If you stay longer, you can take a taxi back to the hotel."

After the confrontation with Lefty, I was too aggravated to have an enjoyable time and ready to leave to escape him.

Macy and Lefty stayed to hang out for a while and take in more of the activities. They didn't care how they got back to the hotel.

I didn't sleep well. I got up at sunrise, went to the lobby, and ordered coffee. I sat at a table and looked toward the door as Lefty and Macy entered. Lefty was so drunk Macy had to hold him up. On second look, Macy wasn't in decent shape either.

They noticed me as a girl brought me coffee. Macy struggled with Lefty and dumped him into one of the chairs. Lefty looked at me and, in a drunken slur, smiled and said, "Hey, Tone." Then he dropped his head on the back of the chair and passed out.

Macy sat down and looked at the steaming coffee. "I could use a cup of that Java, mate."

I got the attention of the girl standing by the desk and pointed to my coffee and then to Macy. She took the hint and went back into the kitchen.

"Looks like you had a wild night."

"It was pretty wild, Mate."

"What did you do?" I reluctantly asked.

"We hung out at that place and for a while Lefty went with one of the girls into the back." Macy hesitated for a second. "Don't worry, I helped him out with it."

I shrugged and asked, "Did you hang out there all night?"

"No. While Lefty was in the back, I met an American, he took us to every strip joint in Managua."

"Glad I wasn't there."

"It was great fun. We missed you, mate."

Lefty was sound asleep when we finished our coffee. "We better get Lefty up to his room," Macy said.

He went over and tried to wake him. Lefty was out cold. Macy spotted a luggage trolley and brought it over. We loaded him onto the cart, his arms and legs sprawled over the edge.

Heading for the elevator, Macy said, "I'm going to grab a shower and rest. Do you mind waking me up before John gets here?"

"Will do," I replied, and shook my head as I watched Macy struggle to get the cart into the elevator.

CHAPTER 10

At nine o'clock, unable to wake Lefty, we left him and went to the dining room for a quick bite before John arrived. Ally entered the room in the middle of our fruit and croissant, walked up to our table, and extended her hand.

"I don't think we've officially met. I'm Ally."

We both stood to shake her hand.

"I'm Macy, this is Tony. Do you care to join us?"

"Thank you," she answered.

"John told us you collaborate with the divers out on the coast," continued Macy.

"That's right. Sounds like you're from England?"

"No, Australia."

"I always wanted to go to Australia."

"Hopefully someday you will."

"Are you from Australia also?" she asked me.

"No, San Francisco."

"That's another place I want to visit."

"Where are you from?" I asked.

"Michigan," she answered. "What are you doing down here?"

"Looking around," Macy answered.

"Isn't there another guy with you?"

"He's sleeping. He had a rough night last night."

She looked at us in disgust, "That's easy to do down here," she snidely commented and stood abruptly. "John should be here any minute. I'm going to go wait for him."

After she left. "Doesn't seem like you're on her most favored list," Macy said.

"I guess not. I don't think your Aussie accent will work on this one."

"Probably not," Macy laughed.

CHAPTER 11

It was hot. John reached over and opened the passenger door. We climbed in the back, and Ally sat up front.

"Where is Lefty?" John asked.

"Still asleep," Ally offered, rolling her eyes.

"Managua disease," John laughed as he pulled away from the curb.

The produce distribution market was on the eastern outskirts of town. We drove through the center of Managua to get there. The streets bustled with activity.

Street vendors galore hawked everything imaginable. Plump women in long dresses heated tortillas over charcoal grills. The aroma of fried chicken legs floated across the area. Nobody seemed bothered by the heat and humidity.

The noise increased as loud Latin tunes came from everywhere. No one took account of drunk men passed out on the street and gutters. The air had the faint odor of cheap rum and urine.

What got my attention were National Guardsmen in starched olive drab uniforms, spit-shined combat boots, shiny green helmets, and automatic weapons slung over their shoulders. People shied around them, not looking into their foreboding dark glasses. Young girls crossed the street to avoid a possible rough flirtation, or worse, being dragged into a secluded alley and molested.

"What's with the soldiers?" I nervously asked.

"Somoza keeps a tight rein on what happens down here to make sure he gets his cut," John answered.

"Don't the people get pissed off?" I asked.

"Yes, but there's nothing they can do about it. If you make too much noise you end up in the volcano."

Ally, unattached to the conversation or the surroundings, looked out the window familiar with the downtown hubbub.

"How do you stay above it?" I asked. "It seems as a newspaperman, you'd be scrutinized by the government."

"There is no government. Somoza considers Nicaragua his hacienda, but needs to look good on the international scene to keep money coming into the country. He tolerates us to keep up his façade."

"Our government lets it happen?" I asked.

"Remember what Roosevelt said, 'Somoza is a son of a bitch, but he's our son of a bitch.'"

"What about you?" asked Macy. "How do you feel about it?"

"I like it down here and I don't want to go anywhere else. At the paper, we choose public interest stories to cover like three gringos coming here to look for gold. Plus, where could I find another Todo Vale, the best little whorehouse in Managua."

Ally jerked her head toward John. "Gross! You asshole. You should be ashamed of yourself!"

"What do you mean?" John laughed.

"You know what I mean, you prick!" she answered with fire in her eyes, ending the conversation.

The produce market was as chaotic as downtown, only more so. The stench of rotting fruit and vegetables and burning trash caused me to gag. In open sheds, the only respite from the sun's heat, trucks loaded and unloaded produce. Crowds of sweaty, filthily clad men, women, and children scurried about exchanging cordobas at a fevered pitch.

Transportation of every kind loaded with produce and sold to local street vendors in nearby towns and villages.

On the market's outskirts were makeshift hovels where these market people lived and raised families in squalor.

I watched the pandemonium and couldn't help but respond, "This is crazy! How do you make heads or tails of this place?"

"It's not as bad as it looks," answered John. "Mafia types take out a space to operate. There is a strong man to control the space and keep out intruders. It gets wild for those who cross the line."

"Like turf wars?" I asked.

"Like turf wars. Shootouts erupt here. It's considered a cost of doing business. To them, it's normal."

"What about the National Guardsmen patrolling, don't they have any influence?"

"They're here to make sure Somoza gets his take. They don't care what happens otherwise."

John changed the subject as he circled around to the back of the market. "Look for a white five-ton ten-wheel International Harvester."

"Is that it, the third shed over?" Macy asked.

"That's it. There's Julio standing on the bed."

Julio was short and stout, white complexioned, with a blue bandana on his head. His jeans were cuffed, metal shank buttons on his western shirt, and he wore cowboy boots. What set him off was the .45 pistol stuffed in the back of his pants.

"Does Julio speak English?" I asked.

"Oh yes, he's from Puerto Cabezas and has family in the States, where he lived for a while. You should get along no problem."

Julio recognized John's car as we drove up, and he jumped off the back of his truck and stood with his legs spread apart and hands on his hips. John greeted Julio with big smiles and an abrazo hug.

"I brought you some customers," he motioned us to come. It comforted us that John and Julio were good friends.

"This is Ally, Tony, and Macy, they're going to need a ride out to Puerto. You going to have room?"

"Sure, mon. I have room plenty. Twenty dollars get them out there."

"There is one more," Ally added.

"That will be four then," looking at the cab of his truck.

"When can we get going?" I asked.

"En la mañana." Julio answered. "Got plenty work to load up before we go."

"You need help loading?" Macy asked.

"Sure, mon, you can help. I leave now, you come with me."

"I better get back to check on Lefty, How do we get with you in the morning?" I asked.

"No problem, I pick you up at hotel four o'clock early, mon."

Chapter 12

John dropped me off at the hotel with a promise to come back later. I went up to Lefty's room. Lefty lay face down on the floor, out cold. I kicked his foot, and he rolled his head up and squinted out a bloodshot eye. "What time is it?"

"Eleven-thirty."

He dropped his head down. "Oh, fuck," and rolled over into a fetal position.

"The truck's here, we're going to leave in the morning."

"Whose truck?"

"Julio's truck. He's loading up today so we can leave at four in the morning."

"Is that chick coming with us?"

"She is. You better get in the shower; you smell like shit."

"I smell like shit?"

"Worse than shit. I'm going down to the bar and get a beer, I'll meet you down there."

I finished my second beer at the patio bar and gazed at the calm swimming pool. A cleaned up Lefty joined me.

"Man! This Nicaraguan rum gets to you," Lefty said.

"Sneaks up on you, does it?"

"More like a freight train. I'm still feeling it."

"You remember what you did last night?"

"This girl took me in the back. Man, was that crazy!"

"Macy said you hit every strip joint in Managua."

"An American guy took us around. None of them were as good as Todo Vale. By the way, where is Macy?

"He's with Julio loading the truck."

"Who is this Julio anyway?"

"Pretty good guy. He packs heat. The best thing about him is he speaks English."

"You say he packs heat?"

"Carries a 1911 Colt .45 caliber pistol in the small of his back."

"Hope he doesn't have to use it while we're with him."

"Me too. There must be a reason he carries it."

"Was that girl with you?"

"She was there, but didn't say much 'til John told her about Vale Todo. She called him a prick for hanging out there."

"Sounds like trouble," said Lefty.

"I'm afraid so," I answered as John joined us at the bar.

"I'll have Old Parr on the rocks," John told the bartender.

"I heard that girl called you a prick?" Lefty teased John.

"Ally, you mean. We know each other pretty well and get along, but she does her woman thing. What most ladies from the States don't understand is that down here prostitution is an honorable trade. You could rob a bank and the police officers might get to it eventually, but if you hurt a prostitute, they'll be on you like stink on shit."

"Why is that?" asked Lefty.

"Everybody has to eat and a lot of these girls support their whole family, mothers and fathers included."

CHAPTER 13

Macy and Julio arrived at the construction materials yard. They got to know one another as they talked about their past. Julio was impressed that Macy was a boxer from Australia since boxing is one of Nicaragua's leading sports.

Julio exited his truck and unlocked a metal box under his seat loaded with cash.

"Don't you get nervous carrying around that much cash?" Macy asked.

"No. That's why I carry this," he answered as he pulled out the pistol.

"Have you ever had to use it?"

"A couple of times, but now everybody knows Julio, 'mon. They know they fuck with me, I'll use it. Nobody wants to die, 'mon."

Inside the store, they went to a chain link cage in the back corner. Julio handed a list through an opening to an older lady sitting behind a black desk.

She looked at the list and walked into the back office.

While we waited for the lady to come back with the prices, Julio asked, "What you gonna do in Puerto, mon?"

"Going up the Rio Coco."

"Up the Rio Coco looking for gold, eh?"

"I heard it's a good place to buy raw gold."

"Plenty gold on the Rio Coco, mon, but rough up there. People go there to look for gold. Some do good and some never come back."

"Do you have any suggestions of getting back safely?"

"You heard of a gringo named Brodie West?"

"John told us about him."

"You get with Brodie, he'll set you straight. Ask him to let Kokie Lampson go with you. He'll get you back."

"Who is Kokie Lampson?"

"Kokie is a Creole boy who works with Brodie now and again. His wife is from the river. He'll take care of you, mon."

The lady came back to the desk and handed Julio an invoice. He pulled out a wad of cash from his pocket, counted out the amount, and passed it through the opening. She called an attendant who went with them to gather the items.

After the lumber yard, they stopped at stores to buy everything from canned goods to bags of used clothing. Macy helped Julio put a heavy tarp over the top of the bed and tie it down. It was after dark when he dropped off Macy at the hotel.

"Be here at four o'clock, mon. We gotta roll plenty early."

"No worries. We'll be ready."

CHAPTER 14

Julio arrived at the hotel on time. He came around and opened the passenger door.

"There is room behind the seat for two and two up front. I need sixty dollars."

"Sixty bucks?" asked Macy. "I thought it was twenty bucks each, so I was expecting eighty bucks?"

"You helped me load the truck; you go for free, mon."

Macy and I climbed in behind the seat, Ally sat in the middle, and Lefty got shotgun.

Four pillows were behind the seat. "Use those pillows to get comfortable. It's a rough road."

Macy and I each put a pillow up against the side of the cab and sat facing each other. An M-1 Carbine rifle stood straight up in a bracket on the sidewall next to me.

"Is this thing loaded?" I asked Julio.

"Always loaded, mon."

"This doesn't seem like a prime vacation spot," I said.

A leather holster was bolted to the dashboard for Julio's pistol. Julio opened the glove box, and another pistol was inside.

He looked at Lefty, "You know how to use this?"

"I know how to use it. I have one at home."

"No worries, mon," Julio said.

He put the truck in gear while Ally calmly filed her fingernails.

The road was good as we traveled down paved Highway 9, but it began to change when we turned right on Route 218. Julio swerved around potholes that got bigger and bigger the further we went until the paving ran out, and we were on a dirt road. He didn't slow down, leaving a cloud of dust.

We came to a washed-out bridge, and he downshifted to descend the bank into a three-foot-deep stream, water coming up to the top of his tires. As we pressed the other side back onto the road, the truck rocked violently to the right, where Ally ended up on top of Lefty. She struggled to get off his lap, and her hand accidentally landed in Lefty's crotch when she was trying to gain leverage. "Ewww," she squealed as she scrambled to get back in the middle seat. She glared at him in disgust.

In a brief time, we came to Mulukuku and pulled up to a roadside café.

It wasn't much, a thatched roof held up by peeled log poles stuck into a cracked concrete floor, but it was shade. A brisk breeze helped keep us cool. Julio was acquainted with the family who ran the place. We sat down at one of the well-worn wooden tables.

Two bare-assed youngsters played in the dirt outside. A plump woman came up to the table and greeted Julio, and they chatted in Spanish. Two older daughters were back in the kitchen, separated from the dining room by a four-foot-high wooden bar top with rawhide and wood stools. They checked out us gringos.

"What's on the menu?" Macy asked.

"Pollo con papas fritas," Julio answered.

"Chicken and French fries," I repeated under my breath.

One of the girls brought out ice-cold Victoria beers.

"You haven't said much on the whole trip," Macy prodded Ally.

Not answering, she cocked her head and raised one eyebrow taking a sip of beer.

Finished with our meal, I commented, "This road leaves a lot to be desired."

"It gets better ahead," answered Julio. "The mining company keeps it up."

"Are we going all the way to Puerto?" asked Macy.

"We stop at Rosita for the night, plenty of places to sleep."

Back in the truck, we waited for Lefty to get another beer.

The road smoothed out, but the truck was too loud to talk, so we took comfort in our thoughts.

I had to ease off Lefty to make the trip bearable. It was my decision to come. Lefty was Lefty, and that's all there was to it.

I was confused about Ally. She had no desire to meld with us. I figured she wanted a ride out to Puerto and didn't have use for us men. I was also concerned about the money we carried. I didn't want to use the carbine rifle sitting next to me.

We entered Rosita after dark, and it was hard to see what the town looked like, with dim street lights illuminating potholed asphalt. Julio stopped in front of a small hotel.

"This is a delightful place for five dollars a night. They have a little kitchen and bar, so you can eat here. I'll be back at four."

Ally looked at him. "Is there another place I can stay?"

Macy and I looked at each other with a slight shock. "Sure," he said.

We stood in front of the hotel, I asked Lefty, "What did you do to her?"

"I didn't do anything to her, Man. She landed on top of me and put her hand on my dick. It wasn't my fault."

"You must have done something?" I said.

"Fuck you, asshole. I need a beer."

While we sat at the bar, I said, "Carrying this money makes me nervous. I wasn't planning to get into a gunfight down here."

"You can't worry about it too much, mate. Julio knows what he is doing, and he carries cash."

"What I want to know is why that chick has to be such a bitch?" said

Lefty.

"I guess we aren't her kind," countered Macy.

"You got that right. She'd feel better around a bunch of poofters."

"You're taking it a bit hard. I think you're getting sweet on her," I added.

"Sweet on her! You gotta be shittin' me. I don't give a shit if she lives or dies."

"That's a bit rough," said Macy.

"Fuck it. I'm going to take a shower and go to bed."

CHAPTER 15

At four o'clock sharp, Julio was in front of the hotel while Ally sat in the front seat.

"You sit up front Tony. I don't want to sit next to that bitch. She doesn't even want to lower herself to stay in the same hotel with us," Lefty said.

"No problem," I answered and climbed in.

Black clouds were ahead with lightning flashes, "Rain come, mon," Julio said as he put the truck in gear.

In twenty minutes, it poured down rain with lightning and thunder like I never heard before. It rained so hard the windshield wipers couldn't keep up. I couldn't see the road but wondered about Julio; he hardly slowed down.

"Can you see the road?" I asked Julio.

"I see it out the side window."

"Out the side window! How do you know someone is not in front of you?" I nervously asked.

"Nobody be out in the rain like this, mon." Julio laughed.

Macy and Lefty were sound asleep; Ally had her knees up and her head resting on her folded arms.

Am I the only one who gives a shit? I wondered.

Julio geared down the truck and braked to a stop. The rain came down in sheets.

"Why did you stop?" I asked.

"Bridge here, mon. I wanna make sure it's not washed away," he opened the door and jumped out.

"Bridge here," I said under my breath, unable to resist checking it out myself.

The instant I got out of the truck, I was soaking wet. The stream raged while six inches of water rushed over the top of the bridge.

"It's good, mon, let's go."

We climbed in soaking wet. Ten minutes later, we were through the storm and rolled down the road under bright blue skies.

With a large stand of trees cut down and dark logs stacked near the road, I asked, "What's going on here?"

"Mahogany, mon, plenty money."

After the grove of trees, the landscape opened onto a large savannah where the road was straight and well-maintained. Julio put his foot on the gas to make up for lost time.

Over a rise, three armed, masked men barricaded a bridge.

Julio slowed down, I looked for somewhere to escape, but there wasn't time or room to turn the truck around.

"Wake up!" I yelled in the back. "We got trouble!"

Macy and Lefty looked out the windshield.

"Oh shit!" yelled Lefty.

We came to a stop. Julio opened the glove compartment, cocked the pistol, and handed it to me. "You use this if you have to. I talk to them and see what they want."

He took his pistol from the holster on the dash and stuffed it in the back of his pants.

I looked at Lefty, who was holding the rifle in his left hand. "Have you ever fired a carbine before?" I asked him.

"I think I can figure it out," Lefty answered.

"Make sure the safety is off before you fire."

"I ain't that stupid," Lefty answered as he took hold of the weapon.

Ally lay down in the front seat.

Julio brazenly walked up to the men and showed no fear as he shouted and waved his hands in the air. He was prepared to pay the tax to cross the bridge, a form of highway robbery Julio had experienced many times. Everyone in the truck was unaware of what was going on and was in full crisis alert.

The men looked at him, and then one of them lifted his mask and showed his face. Julio dropped his hands and raised his head in laughter as the two embraced each other.

I was confused about what was going on but figured the crisis was over.

Julio gestured the men toward the truck and took four beers out of the cooler. In the Miskito language, he pointed inside the cab. The men looked in and waved, and I waved back. They finished their beers and opened the barricade.

Julio climbed in, "That's my cousin."

"Your cousin is a bandit?" asked Macy.

"Sometimes," Julio laughed.

CHAPTER 16

Puerto Cabezas started as an Indian village named "Biliwi" that sat upon a bluff overlooking the Caribbean Sea.

In the early 1800s, the British established a settlement to harvest mahogany and yellow pine, renaming the bluff "Bragman's Bluff" after one of their sea captains. The British eventually claimed the Miskito coast as a protectorate and set up four kingdoms with Miskito kings.

The British lost their dominance when Nicaragua became an independent state. "Bragman's Bluff" was renamed "Puerto Cabezas," after General Rigoberto Cabezas led a campaign to reclaim the Atlantic Coast for the new country of Nicaragua.

In the early 1900s, American timber and fruit companies received a concession called "The Company Times" from the Nicaraguan government to harvest mahogany, yellow pine, and bananas. Life was good on the Miskito Coast as the Americans moved in to convert Puerto Cabezas into a modern town with beautiful white houses, clean water systems, stores filled with modern products, schools, and hospitals. A railroad system serviced outlying lumber mills and banana plantations along with a pier out through the surf to load product onto ships. Good-paying jobs were aplenty for the coastal people known as Costeños.

Trouble started in the 1920s when the rebel General Augusto Sandino targeted American installations. The communist revolutionaries under his leadership drove the Americans out by tearing up railroads, burning bridges and mills, and cutting off the heads of the American managers. The "Company Times" ended.

CHAPTER 17

P uerto Cabezas was a worn-out, dirty town. Aged wooden houses in desperate need of paint lined the streets. The bustling main street led to a pier that juts out into the Caribbean. A small freighter moored to the pier had fishing boats tied or anchored around it. At the foot of the pier is a seafood processing plant. Amid the fishy odor, women dressed in white smocks and hair nets, feverishly fileted fish to be quickly frozen and shipped around the world.

"I'll get out here," said Ally.

I opened the door and jumped down to let her out. She took her bag and left without saying anything.

"What a bitch!" exclaimed Lefty.

The town baseball diamond was the dominant structure along the oceanfront road that overlooked the beach. A crowd gathered in the weedy, trash-infested central park and listened to a young gringo evangelist preach the gospel. The scent of stale urine filled the air. The only place to make calls was at the telephone building next to the makeshift movie house featuring Audie Murphy in "To Hell and Back." The grocery store advertised frozen chicken and ice cream Eskimo Pies posted in the windows.

Julio stopped in front of a sign announcing Dona Alana's Hotel. A drooping mango tree dominated the grassy front yard littered with overripe fruit.

Two mid-sized dogs raced around the corner of the building, viciously barking at us from inside a white picket fence.

The snarling dogs stood by the gate until Julio picked up a rock. They ran around to the back with their tails between their legs.

The well-kept wooden structure had a row of rooms on each side of a covered breezeway. Behind the rooms, a covered cement patio with tables and chairs faced the sea. Colorful hammocks hung from painted posts holding up the roof. Left of the patio was an open kitchen. Above the kitchen were living quarters that looked out over the sea.

A plumpish lady came down the breezeway. She wore a sleeveless pink dress, an orange head scarf, and blue tennis shoes. Her shiny white teeth glistened through bright red smiling lips, making one feel at home.

She recognized Julio's truck and cried out, "Hola, Julio!"

Julio handed her a flimsy present wrapped in brown paper, "Hola, Dona Alana, them boys here need a room."

Briefly, she looked at the package and placed it under her arm, "No problem. Please come in."

"Them are Macy, Tony and Lefty," Julio introduced. "Them good boys, you take good care, you hear?"

"You no worry, Julio. I treat them boys good, you no worry, now," she answered with teeth gleaming.

Julio formally shook our hands before driving off.

Dona Alana led us to the back patio and offered us something to drink. Flower pots engorged with colorful plastic flowers hung from the ceiling. Framed posters of the Swiss Alps decorated the back wall. The dogs lay calmly in the grass. Seabirds soared overhead in the upwelling vortex, scanning the muddy shore for bits to eat.

Lefty chose a hammock. Macy and I sat at one of the tables looking out over the choppy sea. The stiff northeast tradewind kept the flies and mosquitos at bay while we drank our beer.

A gray female tabby cat wandered onto the patio and came directly under Lefty's hammock. Lefty glanced at the cat, reached down, and scratched her behind the ears. With a leap, she landed in the middle of his chest. They stared eye to eye. Surprised by this friendly cat, he continued to scratch its ears. It lay down and began to purr.

Dona Alana watched with concern, "Oh, Mr. Lefty, you must be careful. Those animals them, be kind to you because they know trouble come your way."

"What do you mean?" Lefty asked as he looked wide-eyed at Dona Alana.

"Them animals know, Mr. Lefty. You must be careful," she repeated.

"That's crazy," he answered, tossing the cat down to the concrete.

"No, Mr. Lefty, not crazy, I know them animals."

The cat looked up at Lefty with sad eyes and sauntered off. It stopped long enough to turn her head to take a last glance at him and rounded the kitchen wall.

Dona Alana continued to look at him, stricken with concern

A church bell began to slowly ring. Bong….. Bong….. Bong…..Bong.

Dona Alana looked toward the sound, then back at Lefty with a terrified look on her face.

"What's the church bell going off at this time of day?" Lefty nervously asked.

"Somebody died," she answered, tears ran down her cheeks.

A tangible silence filled the patio as we looked at each other, focused away from Dona Alana.

Freaked out by the vibes, I change the subject, "You know Julio?" I asked Dona Alana, bringing her out of a trance-like state.

She hesitated before she answered, wiped away her tears with the back of her hand, broke her gaze from Lefty, and then sharply turned her head toward me with a smile. "Of course, him, my nephew."

"Your nephew!" exclaimed Macy. "We almost got robbed by a member of your family."

"That be my sister's son, Joaquin. He is a bad boy. Him cause plenty trouble for his momma.

She regained her previous countenance and stood abruptly, "Would you like food now?"

"Yes, please," I answered. "What do you have?"

"I have chicken and salad. Would you like?"

"Thank you, that would be great," I answered.

On her way to the kitchen, Macy asked her, "Do you know where we can find a man named Brodie West?"

"Mr. Brodie? Sure," she looked toward the pier. "He boat is missin.' Him out a *fishinen*."

"You mean fishing," Macy corrected.

"Yes, out a *fishinen*."

Dona Alana sat down with us as we ate and focused her attention on Lefty; he squirmed in his chair, wishing she would leave him alone.

After we ate, she showed us our neatly painted rooms, each with a single bed, clean sheets, a pillow, and a thin blanket on the foot. A mosquito bar hung from the ceiling, ready to use.

"What do people do for night life around here?" Lefty asked.

"Big dance house here, plenty people go there."

"Where is it?" Lefty asked.

"Not far," she answered, pointing in the general direction with her chin.

Out in the night air going to the dance hall, Lefty spoke up, "Wow, man, how weird."

"You mean about the animals?" I asked.

"And the way she looked at me,"

"Pretty freaky, but I feel everything is freaky around here," I answered.

"Don't let it get to you, mate. We'll take care of you," Macy chided, trying to take the edge off.

"I don't need anybody to take care of me. I thought it was weird. That's all."

Macy took Lefty at the back of the neck and gave him a friendly shake, "Come on, mate, let's find this dance hall."

Chapter 18

L oud cumbia tunes led us to the large blue and yellow cinder block dance house. A crowd of people stood outside under the glow of a bare light bulb hanging on the wall.

The dimly lit dance hall had enough light to make out a bar to the right. On stage, between large, stacked speakers, a four-hundred-pound Black man in sunglasses and a full afro worked a turntable and soundboard.

Booming music competed with noisy ceiling fans that cooled sweaty bodies of all ages, sizes, and shapes that gyrated to the Latin/African beat.

We ordered beer and turned to watch the people dance. Down from us, a thin, thirtyish gringo, with an unruly head of hair in a matching green work uniform tugged on a Victoria. His arms draped over a young Miskito girl, not older than fifteen. She leaned against his hip and wore a pink tube top that barely covered her breasts. Skintight baby blue capris covered her legs. Her arms were securely fastened around his waist.

The gringo came over and shouted over the music, "I'M JOHN WAYNE. I HAVEN'T SEEN YOU AROUND. YOU JUST GET HERE?"

Macy took the lead and shook John's hand, "GOT IN THIS AFTERNOON, MATE. I'M MACY AND THIS IS TONY AND LEFTY."

"DO YOU LIVE HERE?" Lefty yelled.

"BEEN HERE FIVE YEARS. TAKE CARE OF THE REFRIGERATION AT THE FISH PLANT. WHERE ARE YOU ALL FROM?"

"ME AND TONY ARE FROM SAN FRANCISCO, AND MACY IS

FROM AUSTRALIA. WHERE ARE YOU FROM IN THE STATES?"

"SOUTH CAROLINA," John answered.

A huge, tall barefoot white man in black Frisco jeans staggered in through the entry door. His dirty white t-shirt hid his overhanging gut. A large Creole woman with the most enormous breasts we'd ever seen draped in an orange flowered muu-muu and worn-out green flip-flops tried to steady him.

"OH, FUCK! NORMAN IS IN FROM THE KEYS, AND HE'S DRUNK. THERE'S GOING TO BE TROUBLE. YOU BETTER BACK UP TO THE WALL," John Wayne yelled as he took hold of his girlfriend and rushed to the back of the stage.

The drunken giant staggered toward the dance floor. He knocked down tables and drinks, and people flew left and right. In the middle of the dance floor, he raised both fists over his head and yelled, "I'M NORMAN STRATFORD. I'LL KNOCK OUT ANYBODY WHO GIVES ME OR SILVIA ANY SHIT!"

He grabbed a fallen chair and heaved it at the speakers, knocking one over and stopping the music.

Girls screamed as people rushed for the exit. We looked at one another, and Macy nodded toward the door, but the crowd blocked our way. Someone turned on the lights inside the dancehall.

John Wayne came around from the back of the stage and yelled, "GODDAMNIT, NORMAN. YOU BETTER KNOCK IT OFF OR THE POLICE WILL BE HERE AND YOU'LL END UP IN JAIL AGAIN!"

"FUCK YOU, JOHN, AND FUCK THE POLICE! I'LL WIPE MY ASS WITH THEM!" Norman screamed and threw another chair at the wall.

John yelled, "SILVIA, WHY DID YOU BRING HIM HERE? GET HIM OUT OF HERE!"

"I told him not to come Mr. John, but him no listen," Silvia shouted back at John.

A horde of police charged into the dancehall. They wore dark blue trousers with light blue long-sleeved shirts. They encircled Norman. He hunched down, clenched his fists, and turned to take on the police.

The police rushed him to wrestle him to the ground. Norman fought them off.

En masse, they rushed and got the better of Norman, took him down, and restrained his arms and legs as they got him in handcuffs.

Norman, when they got him to his feet, lunged at them and yelled, "I'LL KILL YOU SONS OF BITCHES!!"

Outside, John Wayne stood with his girlfriend.

"What was that about?" Macy asked John Wayne.

"Fucking Norman! Silvia tries to keep him out at the keys to buy lobster. Whenever he comes to town he does this shit and ends up in jail. I'll have to go feed him," John muttered.

The police struggled to get Norman in the back of a police jeep. As he passed us, Norman stopped struggling, winked his right eye like it was a game, and started up again until they got him in the jeep and drove off.

"You know this guy?" Macy asked John.

"Of course, I know him. He's one of my best friends. It's when he gets to drinking he does this shit.

"Where is he from?" asked Lefty.

"England," John answered. "He fought with the British forces at Suez. When he got home his brother sent him to Jamaica to run the service department in his Jaguar dealership. He fucked up there so he sent him here to run a dive boat diving for lobster. He fucked that up too, so me and Brodie built him a platform out on the keys so him and Silvia could fill dive tanks and buy lobster. Out there he stays straight."

"Where are the keys?" I asked.

"They're forty miles northeast."

"He stays out there by himself?"

"Yes. Brodie takes him food, ice, and gas for the compressor. Norman trades the divers' lobster for air and Brodie buys the lobster from him."

"Can other people invest in this activity?" Macy asked, always looking for ways to make extra bucks.

"If you want my advice, don't do anything until you get to know your way around. Most people who invest here go home broke in a couple of weeks."

"They carted this guy off to jail. What's the jail like down here?" Lefty asked.

"You don't want to go there. Stupid Norman wears going to jail as a badge of honor."

"What do you mean?" asked Lefty again.

"It's a concrete box with a rod iron roof and door. They don't feed you and if someone doesn't bring you food, you starve to death."

"Where do you shit?" asked Lefty.

"You shit and piss on the floor. They have a water tap with a hose inside, so you can drink and then wash your shit out the door."

"He wears that as a badge of honor?" I asked.

"He brags about the times he's been in jail. He's the nicest guy you ever met when he's sober, but give him a bottle and there's hell to pay."

"How do you get out?" asked Lefty.

"They keep you in for nine days incommunicado, innocent or guilty, to figure out your crime then send you to a judge. In Norman's case, Brodie and I can usually get him out if we promise to keep him out at the keys. Sometimes we slide the police chief a little cash."

"You and Brodie know your way around," said Macy.

"We do, but you must keep your nose clean around here. Brodie is the main player and keeps the economy running for the fishermen. He sails and buys product from the coastal villages. He's a straight shooter, the people trust him."

"What product does he buy?" Macy asked.

"Shrimp, Snook and lobster. He pays cash and sells it to George Morgan at his fish plant."

"You know John Weissman?" Macy asked.

"He's a newspaper man. Him and Brodie have something going on, but I don't know exactly what."

"Weissman told us to hook up with Brodie. Where can we find him?" asked Macy.

"He's at sea. His black hulled sailboat with red sails and yellow trim is named *Creole Princess*. It's anchored south of the pier when he's here. He's not hard to find."

CHAPTER 19

Macy, up early, scanned the ocean for the black sailboat with red sails.

Entranced by a fleet of boats with colored sails that fought through the surf, he asked Dona Alana, who was serving him hot coffee, "What are those boats down the beach?"

Dona Alana looked down the beach, "Those pretty boats them Mr. Brodie build for Alejandro and him brothers at Land Creek. Them go afishenin every day this time. Them bring back plenty fish."

"How far do they go out?"

"Them go out plenty far. Come back late them. Bring back plenty fish."

I joined Macy to enjoy the morning cool with cake, fruit, and coffee.

I looked out to sea and asked Macy, "What do you think our chances are?"

"What do you mean? Like making any money?"

"That and getting out of here alive."

"Are you scared, mate?"

"I didn't think it was going to be a cake walk, but had no idea it was going to be like this."

"Shit, mate we haven't even gotten into the adventure yet. Going up the Coco is going to be the real test."

"That's what makes me nervous."

"Nobody says you have to go."

"No, I'm in. I wanted you to know how I feel. Lefty seems oblivious to anything, and I worry about him."

"Lefty is a good bloke, and he'll do all right. There is only one way to find out."

"I guess you're right," I answered. "Hey look! There's our man."

Around the north point, the black boat under red sails came into view. She was a beautiful sight with a bone in her teeth and a wake on her bow as she charged toward the pier. She rounded the pier, dropped her sails, and threw out the anchor.

"I'll wake up Lefty. We better get down there. I don't want to miss this guy," I said.

"Right, mate."

From the pier, we watched a tanned, well-toned gringo paddle a dugout canoe that served as his dingy. He caught a breaker and surfed the last bit in.

Down on the beach, Macy asked, "Are you Brodie West?"

His weather-beaten face had a deep scar from under his left sky-blue eye to the corner of his lip. He was barefoot and wore frayed cutoff khakis cinched up by a cotton rope. A six-day growth of gray stubble completed the image of a modern-day seadog.

He looked up at us, "The very same."

"I'm Macy McDonald, this is Tony Taylor and Lefty Jackson. John Weissman said to look you up."

"Heard you were coming. Heading up the Coco are you?" Brodie answered.

A green World War II Army jeep interrupted. The driver was a young, thick Creole man in long brown trousers tucked into black combat boots. His neatly pressed blue and white plaid buttoned-up collared shirt gave the air of civility. His broad nose, jovial, bright eyes, and warm white toothy smile drew you to him the instant you saw him.

"Excuse me a moment, gents," Brodie said as he turned to the Creole man. "Hey, Kokie, I have six hundred pounds of product, and I'm short on ice. Run up to the ice plant and fetch us fifty pounds. Bring another ice box on your way back."

As the Créole man drove off, Macy asked, "Is that Kokie Lampson?"

"Yes. How'd you know?" questioned Brodie.

"Julio told us to get with him."

"You'll have time for that. Right now you can help me roll my skiff down to the water."

He led us to a twenty-foot wooden skiff on the sand with an outboard motor on the back. The skiff sat on two small logs.

"Macy, your two buddies can help me push while you throw another roller log under the front as we go."

Eager to help, we rolled the skiff down to the water's edge.

"When Kokie gets back, you can come out with me to help unload the product," Brodie offered, as he checked the gas tank.

While we waited for Kokie to return, Brodie asked, "Julio brought you in, I suppose."

"He did, mate. We got in last night."

Lefty, with a slight smile on his lips, said, "Your buddy got busted last night at the dance hall."

"What buddy?" asked Brodie.

"That Norman dude."

"NORMAN! God damn it! Who brought him in? What did he do this time?" Brodie barked.

"Tore the shit out of the dance hall," Lefty answered.

"That's nothing new, ain't nothing I can do about it now. I have to unload this product. Fresh fish and shrimp can't wait."

Kokie brought the jeep down to the skiff with a large wooden ice box in the back.

"Hey Koke, you hear Norman's in the can!"

"Ya mon, John told me," Kokie smiled.

"If John knows about it, he'll feed him today. Come on, fellas, help me load this box in the boat."

Each of us took a corner of the box and placed it in the middle of the skiff.

"You better take off your shoes. You're going to get wet. Throw them in the jeep," Brodie said as he pushed the skiff into the surf.

Brodie turned to Kokie. "These guys can help me. Go to the fish plant and have Rodriguez bring their truck."

Waist-deep in seawater, we held the skiff into the surf. Brodie dropped the prop into the water. On the second pull, the engine came to life.

"Hop in and hang on!" he commanded as we plowed out through the waves.

The boat leaped over the waves getting us soaking wet. Outside the breakers, we raced toward the black sailboat. On the deck stood Ona with her cutoff jeans that exposed her long, dark, and shapely legs. On her braless chest was a blue and white tee shirt with the "LA Dodgers" logo on the front.

Alongside the black hull, Brodie tossed a line to Ona and lashed the two boats together. Ona pulled a twenty-pound bag of shrimp from the icebox and transferred it to the skiff.

Brodie looked at Macy, "Put ice over the top of these as I toss them in. You two fend off so the boats don't bang into each other."

"Where did this product come from?" asked Macy.

"Sandy Bay, Bismuna, Awastara and Krukira," answered Brodie.

"How often do you go?"

"Twice a week. We take ice up and bring product back."

"How do they catch shrimp?"

"They use a beach seine. They haul the net out with a dugout making a big circle and bring it back to the beach. The villagers pitch in to haul the net. If there are shrimp, there are Snook feeding on them. They take enough to feed their families and the rest they lay up to sell. They know I'm going to be here Tuesdays and Fridays. They pull the seine that morning so I can get it as fresh as possible."

"Do you make good money doing this?"

"In relative terms, I do okay but it doesn't take much to live down here."

Lefty couldn't take his eyes off Ona.

After transferring the product to the skiff, Brodie and Ona put everything in order and locked up the cuddy cabin. We raced to the beach where Kokie and Rodriguez waited. We helped load the truck as Ona dove into the surf and stood up. Her perfectly formed breasts were exposed under the clinging wet tee shirt as she walked off down the beach.

"Tell you what gents, this product must go to the plant, and then I'll try to get Norman out of jail. Let's meet at the Malecon for dinner at five, and we can talk about what you need."

"Where is the Malecon?" asked Macy.

He pointed across the pier to the top of the bluff. "See that covered patio on the bluff? I'll see you there."

CHAPTER 20

Ona glanced at us as we entered the thatched-covered veranda of the Malecon and turned her eyes to the sea.

Brodie broke his conversation with John and said, "Have a seat."

"How's Norman doing?" Macy asked as we sat down.

"Not good. We couldn't spring him. The police are mad at him. He'll have to soak in that hellhole for a day or two."

A heavy-set waiter came to take our order.

"Let us buy the next round of drinks," Macy offered.

"You're going up the Coco looking for gold," Brodie started right in. "People have tried it, but I don't know how they made out. People come down here looking for easy money, but finding easy money here isn't easy."

Lefty broke in and asked, "How did you get down here? You doing all right?"

"It depends on what your expectations are," answered Brodie. "I fought with the Marines at the Chosin Reservoir in Korea. This scar on my face was from a commie grenade. It was so damn cold, I swore I'd never be cold again. I found this place and decided to stay. You take John here. He ran a scallop boat up in South Carolina and ran into woman trouble. Besides being a boat captain, he's a damn good refrigeration man. They needed a good man at the ice plant and took him on."

"How did you end up here John?" asked Lefty.

"While I was out at sea, my wife was having sex with everybody on the docks. When I confronted her, she killed herself. I wanted to escape and heard about an English guy starting a seafood plant down here to launder drug money. He needed a refrigeration man and was paying big bucks so I took the job. Things got scary with guns when I ran into George Morgan's people in Bluefields. They told me there was work here. I caught a ride to Puerto Cabezas, and Morgan put me to work."

"Damn," Lefty said under his breath, slowly shaking his head.

"You come to out of the way places, you find out of the way people," said Brodie.

"What's the situation at the gold mine, I asked."

Brodie took a drink of his beer, "You see that gringo over there, his knee wrapped up. You know what he does for a living?"

I shook my head no.

"That's Charlie McCabe, the assassin. He fought in Korea with the Army 25th regiment, Wolfhounds. You ever heard of Pork Chop Hill?"

"Of course. I spent two years in the Army in Germany. Every soldier knows Pork Chop Hill."

"He was in the middle of it, wounded four times and kept fighting. He came here looking for gold like you fellas and heard about the problem at the mines with the unions. The Canadians who own the mine hired him to assassinate the union leaders, and he does an excellent job of it."

"Can't anybody keep a secret in this place?" Lefty asked.

"No secrets here, gents. You're gringos and everyone knows you're either looking for fish, mahogany, or gold. The minute you head toward Waspam, they'll know you're looking for gold."

"Why doesn't somebody do him in? He's sitting right there. He's not hiding," asked Lefty.

"People have respect for Charlie. It's the Old West out here. Locals respect someone with balls, and Charlie has a pair. Places he goes he's treated like a hero. These Indians are fiercely independent. They feel Charlie is on their side fighting the Spaniards and they don't like Cuban labor organizers."

"Who are the Spaniards?" asked Macy.

"Somoza and the people who live on the Managua side," Brodie answered

Ona silently got up and left. Lefty followed her out with his eyes. Brodie took no notice and kept talking.

"Somoza has nothing these Indians want, and if he respects their way of life, they leave him alone. When it comes to unions, they have no idea what they're talking about. If Charlie pops off a leftist union organizer or two, he's a hero."

Lefty couldn't help but ask, "Your girlfriend, she can't hear or talk?"

"She could talk, but because she never heard a spoken word, she doesn't bother. She watches and notices things nobody else does. She helped me build that boat. I got her a sewing machine, and she made the sails by herself. Like the rest of these people, she's as independent as hell. When I try to help, she gets mad and pushes me away. She is the best sidekick anyone could ask for.

"Does she live with you?" Lefty continued to pry.

"Not officially. She takes care of her ailing mother. She comes and slides in next to me in the early morning."

"Seems like you and her get along pretty well."

"You have to learn about these women. Like I said, they are fiercely independent, you can't put your finger on them. You treat them well, and they'll take care of you." Brodie smiled.

"What about that Ally chick? She is a weirdo," Lefty growled.

"Ally is a doctor and an in–your-face liberal who doesn't suffer fools lightly. She's from a rich family in Michigan and came out here as a Peace Corps volunteer. She saw a need to get a decompression chamber to keep the divers from getting the bends. Out on the keys, she stays on Norman's platform. The biggest problem she'll have with the decompression chamber is to get the divers to use it."

"There's no love lost between us," Lefty added.

"I can understand that. She's totally focused on what she's doing with no time for social life."

"What does she do out there with Norman?" Macy asked.

"She collaborates with the divers on times and depths. They can only stay down so long at each depth. It's not an easy task. The Indians don't like taking instructions from anybody, especially a white woman," answered Brodie. "I have to hand it to her, she's a tough one and won't give up easily."

"We're here and we want to buy gold. What is the best way to go about it?" asked Macy.

"You're not going to be able to go out and buy quantities of gold. If things were different, Charlie over there would be your best bet. But right now, I'd stay as far away from him as possible."

"Why's that?" asked Macy.

"If trouble starts while you're out there, they'll associate you with him and become a target."

"What do we do?" asked Macy again.

"It will take time. You have to build a relationship with the local people and let them do the dealing for you."

"That could take forever," I said in frustration.

"It can, but it depends if you want to buy gold or not."

"How about Ed Thompson?" John Wayne broke in.

"Ed would be a major source of information. He's been out there for thirty years. The problem is finding him," Brodie continued. "My problem with Ed is he came here with the Marines in 1929 and fought against Sandino. One day he left and joined Sandino and began fighting with the other side. I consider him a traitor."

"Why did he do that?" I asked curiously.

"He didn't like the politics of the people he was defending. Now he's so paranoid and hard to find, he thinks the Marines and Somoza are after him. It's driven him crazy. If you ran into him, he won't tell you much."

"What about Kokie?" Macy asked. "Julio said his family might be able to help us."

"His wife's family is from there, but you'd have to take that up with him."

"How much time are we talking about?" I asked.

"At least a week to check out the situation and see if you want to continue. You might find it isn't worth your while."

"We're here," said Lefty. "I think we should go and check it out."

"Fuck!" I said and buried my head in my hands.

Macy finished off his beer. "I think we should go, mate. Nothing ventured, nothing gained." Turning to Brodie, "Where can we find Kokie?"

"Be down at the pier in the morning, you'll catch him there. I've told you all I can, I got to go. Good luck on your venture. I'll see you in the morning."

CHAPTER 21

As we returned to the hotel, I asked, "What do you think? This isn't going to be easy money."

"It never is," said Macy.

"This is a cool place," said Lefty. "Brodie sure has a hot girlfriend."

"Is that all you ever think of?" I said as I shook my head.

"Fishing crab in Alaska wasn't easy either, but I'm glad I did it," said Macy.

"That Charlie dude is weird," said Lefty. "I don't want to hang around with him."

"That's good to hear coming from you," I said.

"What do you mean coming from me?"

"It's hard for me to tell if you take this shit seriously."

"There you go again, asshole. Of course I take it seriously. I want to go out on the Rio Coco and find gold. Is that serious enough for you? That's what we came here for, and that's what I want to do."

As we argued our way into the hotel, Charlie McCabe sat on the patio, drinking a beer. We stood a moment and wondered what to do. Macy took the lead, "Hey mate, Macy McDonald," and held out his hand.

"I hear you are going up the Coco?"

"How'd you hear that?" asked Lefty.

"Overheard it in the restaurant."

"Is that why you came here?" asked Lefty.

"I need help."

"What kind of help?" I asked.

"I need someone to pick up something for me."

"We hear it ain't a good idea to hang around with you," said Lefty.

"That's good advice, but I need help, and I'm willing to pay someone handsomely."

"How handsomely?" asked Macy.

"Five grand."

Giddy with excitement, "Five thousand bucks to pick up something!" exclaimed Lefty.

I sat quietly thinking, This isn't good. Why are we talking to this guy?

Almost unable to control himself. "What is it?" shouted Lefty.

"Personal items."

"Why don't you go get it?" asked Macy.

"I can't go to where it is."

"Why not?" asked Lefty.

"It's complicated. I want to know if you want to make money?"

"What do we have to do to pick it up?" asked Macy.

"Go in and do your business and on your way out stop in Santa Rita and go to the Moravian Church. Ask to see the pastor and give him a note, and he'll give you the package."

"You'll pay five thousand dollars to get a personal item. It must be pretty personal," laughed Lefty.

Charlie stared at Lefty and didn't answer as he slowly sipped his beer with a steady hand.

"How do we get paid?" asked Macy.

"I'll give you twenty-five hundred up front and the rest when you bring it back."

"I'll have to talk it over with my mates," said Macy.

"That's understandable. I'll be here at first light to get your answer."

Charlie finished his beer, stood up gingerly, favored his left leg, and limped down the breezeway out to the street.

We sat around the table and looked at each other, I said. "Well?"

"I'm in," said Lefty.

"Jesus Christ, Lefty! You realize this guy goes around killing people?" I yelled.

"Of course I realize that. He's not asking us to kill anybody, he wants us to pick up a package."

"How do we know what's in the package? Shit man, it could get us thrown in that concrete box or even killed, you fucking idiot," I shot back.

"For one thing I'll have my own money and not deal with the guilt trip you've been laying on me since we started this trip. In fact, asshole, if you're not into it, why don't you pack up your shit and go home. You've been living off the tit of your parents ever since you were in high school, you cunt!"

"You ungrateful son of a bitch!" I yelled, and lunged at Lefty.

Lefty anticipated my move and swung a right that caught me on the jaw. I went to my knees and launched at him with a full-body tackle. We crashed into a table, which opened a gash in Lefty's head. Blood poured down his face, and Lefty got me in a headlock. I pounded Lefty's ribs as Macy jumped up to separate us.

"Knock it off, you idiots!" he yelled, as he pulled us apart.

On my feet, ready to go again, Lefty was covered in blood. Dona Alana watched from her room. She yelled at her daughter, who took off at a run. Lefty lay on the ground and wiped blood out of his eyes. Dona Alana rushed down the stairs with a towel. She pressed part of the towel on the wound and cleaned his face with the rest.

Still hyped up, Macy forced me into a chair. "Give it rest, mate," and held me in the chair.

Dona Alana's daughter was at the end of the breezeway, and Ally was standing next to her with her medical bag.

"Not you! What in the hell have you done?" she said as she knelt beside Dona Alana and looked at the bloody towel.

"A little altercation," answered Macy.

"I guess so," She answered. She lifts the towel to look at the wound. "This is going to take stitches. Do you have alcohol, Dona Alana?"

"Yes, ma'am," running upstairs to fetch it.

"Where can I get stitches?" asked Lefty.

"I can do it. I have a kit in my bag. No Novocain. It will hurt a bit."

"Great!" answered Lefty.

Dona Alana came back down with a bottle of vodka. "I have this."

"Do you know what you're doing?" asked Lefty.

"Done it a million times. I'm a doctor," she said, opening the bottle.

"Can I have a drink of that?" asked Lefty.

"You better take two or three. I need to shave around the cut first and get the bleeding to slow down. Macy, come and put pressure on the wound."

Macy applied pressure while Ally looked into her bag and took out a razor blade.

"I'm not going to ask what happened."

"Best you don't," answered Macy.

She took Macy's towel, poured the vodka on the wound, and shaved around it.

"Ouch!" cried Lefty.

"Take another drink," she commanded.

I watched the operation. "Sorry, Lefty."

"Don't worry. I've had worse," he answered and held out the bottle so I could have a drink.

"Don't drink it all! I'm going to need it," said Ally as she began to stitch Lefty up.

Ally placed a gauze bandage over Lefty's wound. "You need to know Nicaragua and especially this area is a very serious place. If you don't take it seriously, you can find yourself in deep trouble."

None of us said anything as she packed her bag and left.

I hoped Ally's lecture jarred a little sense in Lefty and Macy and asked, "What are we going to tell that guy in the morning?"

"I'm going to tell him I'll do it," said Lefty.

I was speechless when Macy agreed with Lefty.

"I'm in favor of it, mates."

It took me a while before I could answer, "I'll go along, but I don't feel good about it."

CHAPTER 22

The dog's bark woke us up, and Charlie waited on the patio.

"What did you decide?" he asked.

"We'll pick up the package for you," answered Macy.

Charlie took an envelope out of his breast pocket and placed it on the table.

"Here's twenty-five hundred. You get the rest when bring back the package. In the envelope you'll find a note to present to the pastor of the Moravian church."

He stood briefly, looked at us, turned, and left without a goodbye.

Brodie and Kokie worked on the skiff when we walked up. Brodie looked at the patch on Lefty's head. "What happened to you?"

"I cracked my head open, got four stitches."

Brodie grunted and looked at Kokie. "These boys have something they want to talk to you about."

"What's up, mon?"

"We'd like to hire you as a guide up the Rio Coco," said Macy.

"For how long?"

"One week. We'll pay you and your expenses."

"When do you want to go?"

"Tomorrow."

"Three hundred dollars mon. My uncle has a car he can loan but costs you money mon."

CHAPTER 23

The ride to Waspam in Kokie's uncle's 1953 pickup was a dusty trip. Waspam had been a trading point on the river as far back as the Aztecs in the 1500s. It was where European pirates recruited Indians to guide them up the river to attack Spanish gold caravans.

Kokie took us to the Hostel Casa de la Rose. It was a quaint, well-maintained establishment with manicured gardens throughout. The owners celebrated Kokie's arrival as old friends.

We checked into our rooms and walked down the main street to the river. It was clear we were in a prosperous area. The river's edge had twenty-foot dugout canoes for charter. Kokie negotiated with one of the captains for one hundred fifty dollars to leave first thing in the morning.

In a dilapidated old building, a Chinese woman ran a Chinese restaurant and take-out with her petite, attractive daughter. Inside, a dirty old man sat and nursed a bottle of rum with a bloody bandage wrapped around his head.

We entered, and Macy offered his hand to the old man. "I'm Macy and this is Tony and Lefty."

The old man shook hands and didn't offer his name. Hungry for a familiar tongue, he offered, "Have a seat," then waved for the young Chinese girl to bring three more glasses.

The old man poured each of us a healthy dose of rum when Lefty asked, "Wow, what happened to your head?"

He reached up and rubbed the bandage, then threw back his head and drained the glass. He grimaced as the alcohol burned his throat and stared at Lefty with bloodshot eyes. "I haven't figured that out yet."

Confused by the answer, "Do you hang out here a lot?" Lefty asked.

"My girlfriend works here," he nodded toward the young Chinese girl.

How this unkempt old man could land such an impeccably clean, young Asian girlfriend was a mystery.

We were ignorant that we sat before an icon of Nicaraguan history; Lefty couldn't help but chuckle. "What does her mother think of that?"

"I finance this operation…besides, this is Nicaragua," he smiled back at Lefty and took a hit from his rum.

In return, the old man asked us, "What are you doing on the Coco?"

"We're headed upriver to check things out. Have you spent time up there?" Lefty asked.

"I spent thirty years up that God forsaken muddy river, but there has been plenty more before me," as the rum softened his brain.

The old man topped off his drink.

"Thousands of people with gold fever crossed over this land on their way to California. They went up to where you are going and struck it rich."

"What's the problem with that?" Lefty meekly asked.

The rum had taken its toll as the old man leaned forward, extended his neck, and growled, "Because they took what didn't belong to them. Others followed in their wake and caused mayhem, death, and destruction for thousands of innocent people!"

After his dissertation, Lefty tasked, "You ever heard of a Charlie McCabe?"

Something clicked in this old man's mind when he heard that name. He felt the bandage around his head.

The old man abruptly stood up. "I have to go," he said and left with no explanation.

Shocked by his reaction when Lefty mentioned Charlie McCabe, we gulped down our rum and headed to the hotel.

Spooked, I said, "That was a bad gash on his head. Did you see his reaction when you mentioned Charlie?"

Lefty acted unconcerned. "The guy was a weirdo, probably lots of weirdos in these parts." He played it down because he wanted to complete their deal and get paid.

Deep in thought, Macy mumbled, "I think that guy was Ed Thompson."

I turned and looked back at the restaurant. "You think so?"

"It was just some crazy ol' guy," answered Lefty.

CHAPTER 24

The boat pilot filled three gas tanks in the predawn darkness at the river's edge for the upriver trip.

Our money belts contained five hundred dollars for the purchase of gold. Lefty wore a baseball cap to cover his wound.

As dawn broke, the pilot started the 35-horse engine. While the engine warmed up, a local lady came to the boat and asked for an upriver ride. The Captain let her aboard with bags of cargo.

We got as comfortable as possible in the tippy canoe with our packs and the extra cargo to deliver along the way. With all the weight, three inches of freeboard were between us and the river. The pilot's son pushed off and sat at the front to watch for snags, rocks, and sandbars.

The morning was cool as we traveled up the musk-smelling river. Other boats were on the water, going one way or the other to beat the afternoon heat. Life began to awaken on the banks of the river. Young boys fished on rocky outcrops to catch breakfast for their families. The smooth water made it easy to go against the current. People waved as we passed by.

The sun rose above the horizon. It didn't take long to warm up. The flow of the water, the sound of the outboard, and the humidity weighed down the eyes of the passengers. The Captain slowed the engine as he rounded a bend to a small village. He nosed the boat into the muddy shore as Kokie stood up. "Time for lunch."

"Great," said Lefty. "My ass is killing me."

Kokie led us to a small kiosk with a couple of tables and chairs set up out front.

I asked Kokie, "You've been here before?"

"Been here plenty, mon. My wife's people live here in the village."

"What do they do here?" I asked.

"Them people here grow food way back in the jungle."

"Why way back in the jungle?" Macy asked.

"So bad people don't steal it."

"So bad people don't steal it?" asked Macy again.

"Ya mon, plenty bad people here. They steal anything."

"That's encouraging," I said. "What do they grow back in the jungle?"

"Corn, beans and cassava."

"Cassava?" I asked. "What's cassava?"

"It's a root, mon."

"What does it taste like?" I asked.

"Don't taste like nuttin, mon."

"What do they eat it for?" Macy laughed.

"Them people here always eat cassava."

"Do they have any beer here?" blurted out Lefty.

Kokie looked at the lady cooking, said something in Miskito, and she brought us beer.

The lady brought four plates with rice and beans, fried plantain, a chunk of cassava, and two pieces of chicken.

"Is this what we ordered?" asked Lefty.

"Every shop serves the same ting up and down the river."

"Takes away any confusion," I laughed.

Halfway through our meal, Macy asked Kokie. "You know what we are looking for on this trip?

"Brodie says you looking for gold."

"That's right mate. Brodie says the best way is find a local person we can trust buy it for us."

"Mr. Brodie him knows them people here. He won't lie to you mon."

"Brodie says you have family in Santa Rita. Would they like to do a little business? We would make it worth their while?" continued Macy.

"Everybody likes to do business, but buying gold is a heavy ting. I would have to ask them."

"We have to pick up a package at the Moravian Church in Santa Rita," injected Lefty. "Do you know the priest there?"

"I know him. My wife's uncle used to be the pastor. When he retired, he opened the store. You will meet him soon." He looked toward the river, "We got to go. The Captain is ready."

CHAPTER 25

Two local women joined us in the boat for a ride to the next village. I couldn't shake the feeling this trip was not going to end well. Too late to turn back. I struggled to keep these feelings to myself.

As the sun set, the Captain brought the boat up to a village to spend the night. Two boats filled with young men landed next to us. My nerves were at the breaking point, and I wondered who these guys were. We stared at each other. It was clear they could easily overpower us.

The two native women left without a word, avoiding the eyes of us men.

I was relieved when Kokie approached one of the men, gave him a big abrazo hug, and conversed in Miskito. He waved us over to introduce us.

"This is Carlos. He runs the fish plant in Puerto."

After we shook hands, Macy asked, "Who are these people with you?"

"Them here is divers. I'm taking them out to those keys them, to dive for lobsta," Carlos answered.

"You bring them from upriver?" Macy asked.

"Ya mon, they make big money at those keys them," Carlos answered. "What you gringos doing on the river?"

"Looking around," Macy answered.

"Lookin' for gold I wager. If you go to Santa Rita there be big trouble there. You better watch your way."

"No problem mate. We have Kokie along to take care of us."

"Kokie is a good boy, but a lot of shootin' going on up there," he warned us.

Kokie found a wooden framed house still under construction for us to stay in for the night. A new tin roof kept out the rain, but nothing stopped the stinging insects. One of the town ladies brought us plates of rice and beans, fried plantain, and a piece of chicken. We offered to pay, but she refused.

While we ate, I brought up the subject, "Fellas, we're in over our heads. I'm scared shitless and think we ought to pull out."

"The situation looks rough," Macy admitted. "But I don't think we ought to pull up stakes yet."

"We can't quit now!" blurted out Lefty. "At least we got to get that package and the rest of my… I mean our money."

"I'll tell you what. You can have my share of the money. Would that make you feel better?" I said.

"I don't see what it would hurt to get the package and see if Kokie's family could buy gold for us. We have to play it cool and stay loose."

Macy broke in, "Lefty is right. This is going to take longer than we thought, but we've come this far. Besides, I plan to stay down here and feel my way around."

"You guys are crazy. I have a bad feeling about this. I barely slept on the hard wooden floor with rats the size of cats that scurried around. I AM FREAKED OUT! I'd love to get the hell out of here." But deep down I knew this was a one-way trip and with no boats going back.

The next day, we were back on the river at dawn for a six-hour boat ride to Santa Rita. The boat weaved around big rock outcrops. Topless native women in sarong-like skirts pounded the family laundry on the rocks. They scarcely looked up as we passed. No one waved now. We entered an unforgiving world where the only rule was the price of gold.

We rounded a bend to see a large settlement with corrugated tin roofs on the shore. Soon, we arrived at Santa Rita.

The Captain nosed in between other canoes to a small pier. His son tied off the boat while we pitched in to move the cargo boxes forward and place them on the dock.

Chapter 26

Compared to the other villages, Santa Rita was a real town. A few cars and trucks lined the main street, which featured shops, restaurants, a hotel, and a gas station. One could hear the hum of a power plant that provided electricity.

We passed in front of the Moravian church as Kokie led us to his uncle's store. Wheelbarrows, rolls of wire, and bags of cement were out in the front. The living quarters were overhead. Kokie's aunt screamed inside as she ran toward him, giving him a smothering hug.

Kokie's uncle heard the screams, and he and his two sons came out from behind and joined the celebration. We quietly looked on.

Kokie introduced us to his family. They extended a gracious welcome and invited us upstairs to the living quarters.

To our relief, Kokie's uncle spoke the King's English and asked why we were there.

Kokie cut straight to the point. "These boys are here to buy gold."

"Many people come here to buy gold," Kokie's uncle said. "Right now, buying gold is a risky business."

Macy stated, "We hear the best way to buy gold is in business with a local person. If you were willing to do business, we'd make it worth your while."

"It's hard to get quality gold. We use flour gold of lesser purity to barter for goods at the store. Good gold is further up river where the Hondurans control the buying and processing. The Hondurans are a rough bunch and people are afraid of them," said Kokie's uncle. "I don't recommend dealing with them. They will cheat you."

Convinced that this whole trip was a waste of time and money, I wanted to get out of there. I was amazed that Macy kept asking questions.

"Do you have any panned gold I could look at?" asked Macy.

Kokie's uncle spoke to his son in Miskito. The boy came back with a small leather pouch. He dumped the contents on the table. The gold mixed with iron oxides looked like dried mud.

"This gold is ten dollars an ounce, the mercury purified button gold gets twenty an ounce."

Macy looked at me and Lefty, "I could get thirteen dollars for this."

I rolled my eyes when Lefty said, "That's better than nothing."

"Can I buy fifteen hundred dollars' worth?" Macy asked.

This made me nervous. I didn't have the stomach for what took place, and I questioned my own sanity about getting involved in the first place.

"It will take me a while to put it together. Do you mind waiting?"

Macy looked at his watch. "No, take your time. We need to get something to eat. Where do you suggest we go?"

"Across the street is a restaurant Come back after you eat."

Kokie stayed with his family. We ordered beers and knew we didn't need to look at the menu. They served one dish.

"What are we going to do now?" I asked, hoping they would see things my way.

"I see potential here," Macy answered. "It's not what we heard, but we have a good deal with Kokie's family. I know everything seems screwed up with this union bullshit, but that will change with time. It's a good opportunity to lay groundwork for the future."

As Macy spoke, men with sidearms approached the street to patrol. Two of them sat at the table next to us and ordered a beer. I made eye contact with one of them, and they stared back until I turned away. They looked at me, not saying a word to each other.

"How do you blokes feel about it?' Macy concluded.

"I like it down here," answered Lefty. "I want in on it."

"We're in deep shit," I answered. "Don't look around, two guys sitting behind you are staring at us. Other guys are roving around the street."

We ate in silence and tried to be as nonchalant as possible. After we paid the bill, the two men watched as we crossed the street.

Lefty said, "We gotta get that package from the church."

"We'll close this deal, get the package and try to get going tonight," Macy said.

After seeing the armed men, Macy realized we were in real danger. For the first time, I saw he was frightened. It only heightened my feeling to get the hell out of there. I wanted nothing to do with this deal.

Back in the store, Kokie and his uncle led us upstairs. On the table were three leather bags of gold. When I saw the three bags, I realized the gold was within reach, and now it was real.

Once the transaction was complete, Macy looked at Kokie. "We want to head back as soon as we pay a visit to the pastor. Do you know where the boat captain is?"

"No, but I can look. They don't travel the river at night."

"Tell him we will pay him well. It's important we get back as soon as possible." Macy looked at his host. "Do you mind if we leave the gold here for now?" He was not sure what might happen out in the street.

"Of course, no problem," Kokie's uncle answered.

CHAPTER 27

Kokie led us to the Moravian Church. The two men at the restaurant followed.

I watched them out of the corner of my eye. "We're being followed."

Behind the church was the parsonage. Kokie went to the porch. The pastor came out and greeted him warmly. Macy presented the letter to the pastor. He read the letter and told us to wait.

He returned with a tightly rolled piece of cracked leather securely tied with a stiff rawhide strap. Lefty asked, "What's this?"

"The letter says I am to give you this package," the pastor said. Lefty placed it in his pack.

Macy told Kokie to tell the captain they were ready to leave. It would soon be dark.

While we sat on the church steps, two men joined the others as they talked and looked in our direction. Instinctively, we knew we were in deep trouble as Lefty held his pack closely to his chest.

In the next few seconds, we would be struggling for our lives. My Army training kicked in with an adrenaline rush. The adrenaline calmed me and set my senses on high alert. I wasn't going to let these guys get us without a fight.

"What do you think we ought to do?" Macy asked. "I think I can take two of them."

"It's not a good idea," I said. "There might be more watching, probably armed."

"I got a .38 caliber revolver," Lefty informed us.

Macy and I looked at him, surprised. "Where did you get that?" I asked.

"Kokie got it for me."

"Where is it?" asked Macy.

"Down in my pack."

Adrenaline charged through my veins. "There's no way we can beat these guys. The only option is to run for the boat and shove off – captain or no captain. Grab gas cans off other boats. We are going to need as much as we can get."

The men moved in our direction.

"It's time to go!" I yelled and jumped to my feet, sprinting for the boats. Macy and Lefty followed behind.

The men rushed after us. Two shots rang out from the corner of the church that stopped their pursuit of us. They hit the ground to take cover. We kept running toward the dock.

Someone ran towards us, favoring his left leg. He pointed his pistol at the two men lying on the ground. They didn't dare move. Who was this person?

We jumped aboard the boat. I went to the engine and pulled the starting cable. The engine started right away. Lefty and Macy grabbed gas cans from other boats and jumped aboard as the stranger caught up and came aboard also. To our amazement, Charlie, the assassin, was holding a Colt 45 pistol.

"What are you doing here?" yelled Lefty.

"Don't worry about it," yelled Charlie. "We've got to get out of here or they'll kill us."

Macy pushed the boat off the dock as another figure raced towards us down the beach. Charlie raised his pistol to fire.

Macy yelled, "Don't shoot!! That's Kokie."

Macy held up the boat until Kokie jumped aboard. He held three bags of gold. We pushed off.

"Captain said he's not leaving until the morning!" Kokie yelled.

"Fuck him!" I yelled, put the engine in reverse, and backed out into the current.

I gave the engine full throttle and raced downriver. Six men, brandishing pistols, boarded a boat to give chase. Charlie fired a couple of rounds to slow them down; two of them fired back. Life-or-death combat was on. We had to beat these guys to Waspam.

More rounds came our way, and one slammed into the transom, barely missing the engine. Splinters went flying as one penetrated the side of my hand, deep into my palm and little finger. I shook off the sting as the two-inch spike of wood entered. Due to the adrenaline rush, I pressed ahead. Charlie fired back as we crouched forward to avoid the incoming bullets.

Their boat pulled away from the dock. I raced the engine to increase the distance between the men firing at us.

The further we went, the darker it became. My biggest fear was running into a sandbar. I yelled ahead to Kokie at the bow of the boat to keep an eye out for obstacles, and I kept the throttle wide open. With the engine's noise and the darkness, I had no idea how far back our pursuers were.

What was Charlie doing in Santa Rita? Why did he follow us if he paid us to pick up the package?

Lefty reached into his pack, placed his pistol on top, and stuffed the leather package down to the bottom.

The first sandbar came on with a thump to the bottom of the boat. We had enough momentum to slide over the top, scraping the bottom and giving full throttle to the engine.

We ran for hours, unable to speak; guided by the opaque shadows of the jungle shoreline, the engine began to sputter. I lifted the gas tank and gave it a shake.

"OUT OF GAS!" I yelled.

As the engine died, I detached the gas line from the empty tank and threw it in the river. Then, reaching forward, I pulled the fresh tank back and inserted the gas line.

In the quiet, Lefty looked at Charlie, "What were you doing in Santa Rita?"

"I wanted to make sure you got the package."

"Why didn't you get it yourself?"

"Because I paid you to get it."

"It would have been nice if you had told us we could get our asses blown off."

Charlie looked at Lefty with a scowl; he didn't offer an explanation.

Before I started the engine, we listened for sounds from upriver. We heard the faint sound of an engine and knew who it was. Our engine started on the third pull of the cord. In the dawn light, we could see rocks ahead.

With enough light to negotiate around the rocks, we got the first look at the other boat behind us. The other boat was gaining on us. It was a matter of time. I had to get as much out of this boat as I could. Pain set in my right hand. I glanced at the wound. It was too deep to try and get out now. I had to bear down and take the pain.

The other boat came close enough to shoot at us. We heard the pop of pistols.

Kokie signaled sand bars ahead. I didn't dare slow down. Charlie fired a couple of rounds. Kokie waved to turn sharply to the right. I swerved in time to miss the sandbar into deeper water.

The other boat fired on us, and more rounds whizzed by.

"FUCK!" Charlie yelled as a bullet slammed into his shoulder and splattered a chunk of flesh into the river. He grasped his shoulder, blood oozed between his fingers.

Kokie yelled, "They ran aground!"

They stopped dead in the water, and the crew was thrown out of the boat into the river.

This was our chance, I yelled up to Kokie, "HOW FAR TO LEIMUS?"

"NOT FAR, GO MON!" he yelled back.

I didn't know how far "not far" was, but Charlie did.

We rounded a bend, out of sight of the other boat, when Charlie yelled at me, "Pull the boat over there," as he waved the pistol in front of my face and pointed to the Honduran shore with his bloody hand.

Lefty reached into his pack and held his pistol under the flap out of sight.

On the Honduran shore, Charlie stepped onto the beach. He pointed his pistol at Lefty. "Now give me that package!"

"Fuck you!" Lefty shouted. "I'll give it to you as soon as you give me the other twenty-five hundred, asshole!"

"I'm not fucking with you," Charlie snarled as he pointed the pistol right in Lefty's face. "I'll blow your fucking head off!"

"Lefty!" I shouted. "Give him the package!"

"Not till he gives us the rest of the money!"

Lefty pulled out his pistol and aimed it directly at Charlie, which caused a standoff. I gunned the engine as they both fired. They missed each other by inches. Lefty lurched back, lying flat on his back by the boat's momentum, unable to wrestle himself back up to take another shot.

Charlie tried to fire again, but the slide on his pistol locked back. His magazine was empty.

Charlie scrambled up the riverbank, "We'll meet again soon, you sons of bitches!"

CHAPTER 28

Around the next bend, a local lady with two children tried to flag us down for a ride to Waspam. Kokie yelled back, "Go to the lady. I have an idea."

When we got to the lady, Kokie talked to her in Miskito. "I told her we have to get out here, but she can take the boat to Waspam and leave it on the beach."

With no other option, we jumped out and handed over the boat. The lady with the two kids was excited as we climbed up the bank and melted into the jungle cover. We watched our pursuers speed by. They didn't take notice of the family in the boat.

Macy broke out in a nervous laugh. "What do we do now, captain?" We laughed uncontrollably as our tension eased.

I've regained control of myself. "We have to get to the road and make our way to Waspam. When they get there, they'll notice our boat is not there and will come back and look for us. Somehow, we gotta get to the truck we left in Waspam. We'll work our way close and then wait until dark before we go into town. Kokie, do you know the way to the road?"

"Come," Kokie answered, struggling to work his way through the thick underbrush.

We stumbled over exposed roots, and vines grabbed our legs and hips. The thick green underbrush with spiders the size of a man's fist hung in the middle of perfectly designed webs. Startled five-foot iguanas crashed through tangled layers of jungle. Sweat poured down our faces into our eyes and pooled in the nape of our necks. Sharp, thorny branches cut into exposed flesh, causing blood and sweat to flow down our arms. Hordes of insects swarmed around, taking advantage of a free lunch.

Lefty asked, "Are there snakes here?"

"Plenty snakes here."

"What kind of snakes?"

"Worse kind of snakes, mon."

"Great!" I cried and almost knocked myself out when I slapped a big green fly, taking a chunk of flesh out of my cheek.

We reached the road and huddled up. I looked at Kokie and said, "How far is it to Waspam from here?"

"Not sure, mon, this road goes around."

Across the road was an open landscape, unlike the heavy brush we came through. I asked, "If we go straight across this field, would we run into the road on the other side?"

"Ya mon."

"How far do you think," I asked.

"Not far."

"Not far, of course!"

Lefty noticed my wounded hand for the first time. "Shit man, what happened to your hand?"

I looked at my hand, "Splinter from when the bullet hit the transom."

"Splinter hell!" said Lefty as he inspected the wound. "That's a sizable chunk of wood. Serves you right for cracking open my head."

I laughed, then brought up another point, "We do have another option," I suggested.

"What's that," asked Macy.

"We have the package. That's what they want. Let's give it to them and get out of here."

"Fuck that!" shouted Lefty. "I got the package and I have the gun. I ain't giving it to nobody. I know it's worth something or these guys wouldn't be willing to die or blow somebody away to get it."

"That somebody might be us," I said.

"It could be," answered Lefty. "But I say we try to get out of here first before we give it up."

"What's so valuable about that package? Open it up so we can have a look," said Macy.

"It's staying in the bottom of my pack and nothing gets opened until we get somewhere safe."

"I wanted to know if it was worth the trouble."

Lefty changed the subject. "I'm dying for something to drink."

Dark clouds formed up behind us and came our way. Sounds of thunder filled our ears.

"It won't be long by the look of those clouds; we'll get drenched. Let's get moving," I commanded.

A fierce wind hit first, then a biblical downpour. The heavy rain drenched our bodies and cooled us off from the blazing sun. Cool water flowed over our faces and arms, washing off sweat and blood. We cupped our hands and drank in as much as we could. The storm ended as quickly as it hit us, and we continued our trek and felt refreshed.

Even though we were tired and hungry, we dared not stop.

CHAPTER 29

At one thirty in the morning, on the outskirts of Waspam, we could see the lights of the disco as music pounded from inside. People milled around by the front door.

My hand throbbed with pain.

Hunched down together in a darkened lot, I asked Macy and Lefty, "Do you remember how to get to the hotel?"

"I think so," returned Lefty.

"Kokie, you go first, and we'll follow you at a twenty-five-yard distance one at a time. Stay out of the lights if you can. We'll meet in the back of the hotel. Act natural. I'll go last."

Kokie nonchalantly shuffled down the street. When he went the distance, Macy followed Lefty. I took the rear. We met behind the hotel.

Kokie knocked on the owner's door and woke him and his wife. When the man came to the door, they spoke in Miskito.

Kokie turned around. "Sit in the veranda, he be right out."

The man and his wife came out in housecoats and joined us.

Kokie looked at the man and his wife. "We being chased by bad people who want to kill us."

I showed them my hand, "This came when a bullet that hit the transom on the boat, and a huge sliver of wood slammed into my hand."

"Things are dangerous right now," he told us. "Ed Thompson was murdered the other night?"

"Murdered!" I blurted out. "Do they know who did it?"

"No, he was shot in the head with a .45-caliber bullet."

The only person we knew with a .45 was Charlie McCabe.

"What can I do to help?" the innkeeper asked.

"We need gas, food, and water. We'll pay you for it," I said.

The man took a rubber hose and bucket, went to his car, and siphoned gas into the bucket.

His wife made sandwiches and added plantain chips and cake.

Kokie started the truck. They wished us luck. Lefty was in the cab; Macy and I were in the back. Out on the road, we turned left toward Puerto Cabezas.

CHAPTER 30

A car was parked two hundred yards outside of town in the middle of the road. Three men with weapons were waiting for us.

"Big trouble ahead," Kokie shouted.

Kokie slammed on the brakes, threw the truck in reverse, and swung around in the gravel. We raced back into town.

"WHAT'S GOING ON!" I yelled.

"GUYS WITH GUNS ARE BLOCKING THE ROAD!" yelled Lefty.

Three shots rang out. One bullet shattered the driver's side rear-view mirror. Lefty leaned out and fired a shot to let them know we were armed.

Kokie negotiated around people milling about the disco. Going full speed, he fishtailed right onto a road heading out of town.

"What are you doing!" yelled Lefty.

"Going to Sandy Bay to get a boat and take it to Puerto," he yelled back.

I yelled into the cab, "What are we doing?"

Lefty yelled, "Going to Sandy Bay to get a boat and take it to Puerto."

I looked at Macy. "We're going to Sandy Bay to get a boat and take it to Puerto."

"Yeah mate, I heard him."

The road was decent, and we sped along. I wondered how long it would be before they came after us.

In the early morning light, we came to a rise and looked back to see a long trail of dust. Someone was on our tail. We assumed it was the Union boys.

The chunk of wood in my hand was too deep to pull out. It needed to be cut out.

Kokie and Lefty were in deep conversation. They yelled over the engine noise. I heard them talking but couldn't understand what they said. I looked back; the cloud of dust was gaining on us.

Sandy Bay on the Kokura Lagoon was a fishing village. Its raised wooden homes protected the occupants from wild animals, snakes, and yearly floods. Small groves of mango and cashew trees peppered the area.

Kokie didn't slow down as we entered the congested village. The wild entry halted a soccer game on the village green. He slammed on the brakes and lost control. The truck slid on the moist grass beside a stilted house near the water. A woman screamed and pulled her three naked children out of the way as we came to a spinning stop. A man worked on an outboard motor and stood motionless with a confused look. Kokie jumped out of the truck. There was quick, friendly recognition as Kokie excitedly spoke in Miskito.

Kokie turned to us. "Mr. Brodie was here last night buying fish. He left early this morning. My friend will take us to catch up with him. He is not far away but we got to hurry. Them boys come soon."

We ran to the water and loaded aboard the boat. Twenty-five miles an hour, wind gusts blew across the white-capped lagoon. As we set out, spray broke over the bow and began to fill the boat. Our clothes and faces soaked, and we wiped stinging salt water out of our eyes.

Kokie yelled, "You have to bail, mon! Bail hard!"

We scooped water with cupped hands to keep the boat from swamping. The water calmed on the leeward side of the lagoon when we entered the two-mile outlet lined by stilted mangrove roots.

The other car drove up, and we witnessed the surreal drama. Car doors flew open, and four men charged out waved weapons and shouted at the people. A small group of villagers huddled together at gunpoint. The final view of the village was a man violently forced down to the boats.

As Kokie watched, he glanced at me expressionless. Our trouble was far from over.

Our boat reached the river mouth where we saw the red sails of the Creole Princess heading south outside the breaking waves. As we approached the sand river bar, we were held back by the heavy breaking surf that pounded the bow of the boat. We fought through the avalanche of churning white water and cascading waves. The boat jettisoned airborne before meeting larger waves ahead.

A massive rogue wave knocked the boat sideways to the waves. The following breaker flipped over the canoe into the surf. Disoriented, we bobbed to the surface, the waves crashing on top of us. Luckily, Lefty wore his knapsack on his chest, which gave him floatation. Macy and my knapsacks were lost in the surf. We took hold of the overturned canoe to get our bearings. Another wave ripped it from our grasp. We swam for the beach as the pursuing boat came on fast. Our feet touched the sandy bottom as we struggled to make it to shore.

Exhausted, we pulled ourselves up to the beach. The pursuing boat ran up on the beach only yards behind us. The men bolted out, gave chase, and fired shots. Lefty rose to his knees, took the wet pistol out of his soaking pack, and fired back. Our pursuers stopped and headed for cover once they realized we were armed. We got to our feet and ran over the hard-packed sand at the water's edge.

Brodie, on the Creole Princess, heard gunshots coming from the beach. He looked back through his binoculars, recognized Kokie and saw that we were in danger.

More shots were fired. Lefty dropped to the ground. "I'm shot in the leg!" he yelled.

Macy and I ran back to help him. Macy took the pistol and fired to slow the rapidly oncoming assailants.

Brodie saw the action and made gestures to Ona. She untied the line that towed the dugout tender and paddled toward the beach. Brodie ducked into the cuddy cabin and came out with his old USMC .30 caliber Browning Automatic Rifle.

He steadied himself against the gunwale and fired three round bursts, which kicked up the sand. The assailants ran for the brush. They were no match for that kind of firepower.

Ona maneuvered the canoe to the sandy beach. We lifted Lefty and placed him in the canoe. Blood ran down his pant leg. The canoe had only enough space for Ona and Lefty.

"We have to push!" Kokie yelled out.

We pushed the canoe through the surf until the water was over our heads. Kokie, Macy, and I swam as hard as we could toward the *Creole Princess*.

Brodie brought the *Princess* outside the surf line. He kept an eye out for activity on the beach with his Browning at the ready. We fought through the surf to reach Brodie. Ona paddled hard and managed to keep the canoe upright.

Shots rang out from the brush line. Brodie peppered the area where the shots came from. The .30 caliber rounds silenced them.

"Fire superiority," Brodie muttered.

Ona brought the canoe to the leeward side of the *Princess*, where she and Brodie muscled Lefty on board and laid him down in the cockpit. Kokie, Macy, and I took hold of the rail and hoisted ourselves onto the deck. Once aboard, Brodie tightened the sails as Ona took the helm. Soon, we were out of pistol range and in the clear.

Our attention turned to Lefty and his bloody leg. Brodie ripped away his pants and exposed his wound; the bullet punched deep into his right hip, and the blood oozed out.

"Is it bad?" asked Lefty in a weak, trembling voice.

"I've seen worse. You'll live," answered Brodie as he pressed hard against the wound to stop the bleeding.

Lefty began to shiver uncontrollably. Brodie recognized the first signs of shock and told Macy to bring a blanket from the cabin. He raised Lefty's legs to get blood back to his heart and brain and covered him up to get him warm.

With Lefty stabilized, Brodie turned his attention to us. "It looks like you had quite an adventure," he said.

"To say the least," I answered and showed him my wounded hand.

Macy leaned back in the corner of the cockpit and stared at the beach. "We lost our kit in the surf, mate."

Our lost gold was the least of my concerns.

"What the hell happened?" asked Brodie.

While we sailed in the stiff breeze, doing nine knots, headed east, I began to explain to Brodie.

He listened intently, then stopped me, "Charlie and his wounded shoulder. Was it life threatening?"

"I don't know, it was bleeding pretty bad, but he didn't have a problem when he scurried up the bank, gimp leg and all.

"I see," he said, squinting his eyes. "Then what?"

When I finished, Brodie paused and mulled over what he heard.

"Those Sandy Bay villagers are well armed, and the union people will have a tough time getting out of there. This story will be up and down the coast in two days. If I take you back to Puerto, you'll be in a world of trouble."

Then he added, "I dropped Ally off at Norman's platform in the keys. We'll go there and she can take a look at Lefty, and we'll figure out what to do after that. Do you have the package?"

"Lefty has it in his pack."

Lefty lay in the cockpit, his face white as a sheet, uncontrolled shivering as he stared at the sky. "How are you doing, mate?" Macy asked.

"Feel like shit," he answered, then turned his head into the cockpit to vomit his guts out.

Macy held Lefty's shoulder until his final wretch, "We're going to the keys, mate. Ally is there and she'll fix you up."

Lefty spit out the vomit residue, then closed his eyes, turned his head up right, dribbled putrid saliva out of the corner of his mouth.

Brodie went forward and came back with a jar, opened it, and, with a spoon, scooped out a small amount of white powder.

"Here suck on this," as he placed the spoon in Lefty's mouth.

It didn't take long for Lefty to say, "Oh yeah," and enter another world.

"What was that?" I asked.

"Opium."

As we moved away from the beach, the *Creole Princess* heeled over with billowed sails and raced toward the Miskito Keys.

CHAPTER 31

Two dark lumps appeared on the horizon. Under a clear blue sky, pelicans and sea birds dove into the static sea for lunch. Pelagic fish dove up from the bottom and leaped through the surface with small mullets in their teeth.

As we approached the two large islands, green mangroves and 30-foot trees became visible. Multiple coral reefs were awash below the surface, and the water became calm like a lake as the reefs sheltered them from the heavy swell. Indigenous, wooden sloop-rigged catboats tied off to lodges on the reef for use by the local fishermen and divers.

Ona stood on the bow and directed Brodie through the maze of coral. We spotted Norman's 30 by 12 foot well-anchored platform atop twin wooden dories beside a reef. A raised galvanized roof covered the small shelter that protected Norman from the weather.

Brodie dropped the sails, rounded up, and eased next to the platform.

Norman took the lines and tied off the boat. "Where did you pick up this crew?" he excitedly asked, with a grin on his face.

"In a shootout on the beach," Brodie answered.

"Bloody hell!" Norman's expression changed to concern.

"I got a wounded duck on board. Where's Ally?"

"She is out with a couple of divers. You can see their canoe next to the outer reef."

Brodie looked at Ona and then gestured toward the canoes. Without hesitation, she untied the canoe and began to paddle.

"What happened," Norman asked as he helped lift Lefty onto the platform.

"They had a run in with union goons up the Coco, who chased them back to Sandy Bay. I picked them up there after a shootout on the beach. Lefty has a bullet in his leg."

"Bloody hell," Norman repeated. "Lay him down on the bed. What was so damn important to go up there and get your ass shot off?"

"They went to buy gold and pick up a package for Charlie."

"For fuck sake!" cried Norman. "Every dumb ass on the coast knows not to get involved with Charlie."

"These here are rookies," answered Brodie. "I'd say they learned their lesson."

"I guess so. Let's have a look at the bullet hole," said Norman.

Norman put on his glasses and then bent down to look at the wound. "Not so bad. Depends how deep that bullet is."

He felt around the wound. "He's pretty docile for one who has a bullet in him."

"I loaded him up with opium," answered Brodie.

"How are you feeling?" Norman asked Lefty.

"Pretty damn good," Lefty answered. "You got any more of that powder?"

Ona reached the platform and Ally leaped on board in her bikini. She glanced around and noticed Tony and Macy, and she tossed down her fins, mask, and snorkel.

With a disgusted look on her face, "What's going on now?"

"We have one with a bullet in his hip," said Norman.

"Jesus, what a bunch of idiots," as she stared at me and Macy.

She checked the wound. "I'm not even going to ask what happened. Norman, put on hot water, I'm going to see how far in that bullet is. What do we have for alcohol?"

"Flor de Cana," answered Norman.

"I'm going to need some towels."

"Help me lift him so I can get this towel under him," she commanded.

Macy and I lifted Lefty up, and Ally noticed the wound in my hand. "What happened there?"

"You sure you want to know," I answered.

She looked up at me in disgust, poured rum on her hands, and washed it around. Then, she inserted her finger into the bullet hole.

"This might hurt a bit."

Lefty moaned as she felt around inside his wound.

She pulled out her bloody finger, and the wound began to bleed. With a corner of the towel, she pressed down hard. "Hold this here," she told me.

She stood up and washed her hands with warm water. "It's in about an inch."

"Can you get it out?" asked Macy.

"It would be better in a hospital," she answered.

"We're not going to a hospital," I answered.

She looked at me again. "I can get it out, but it's not going to be easy. What's he on, anyway?"

"Opium," answered Brodie.

"You better give him a bit more."

She poured rum around the wound. "Is that water boiling?" she asked Norman.

"Yes ma'am."

"Put two metal teaspoons in it and let it boil for a minute."

She brought out forceps in her medical case and placed them in boiling water.

"Tony and Macy, I'm going to need your help. Wash and sterilize your hands with the rum."

"What do you want us to do?" asked Macy.

"I'll get to that. Brodie give him some more opium, but not enough to kill him."

Brodie went to his boat as Ona and Kokie watched from a distance.

"Brodie, you, and Norman are going to have to hold him down. Tony and Macy, you will take the handles of the spoons. One on each side, insert them into the wound and spread it open, I'll go in with the forceps and when I get a hold of the bullet, we come out together. Don't come out until I tell you, you got that."

"Yes ma'am," we answered sheepishly.

"OK Brodie, give him some more opium."

She placed a clean towel down next to the boiling water and, with a fork, pulled out the forceps and held it up to cool. She picked out the spoons with forceps and handed one to Macy and me.

"OK, here we go. Hold him down. You get on either side of me but give me room to work. Go ahead and put in the spoons."

"A little deeper," she told us. "Now put on side pressure to open it up."

With the forceps, she took hold of the bullet and wiggled it back and forth until it began to move.

"Here we go now, slowly out." After a final pull, out came the bullet. She held it up and dropped it in the boiling water. "He might want to keep this."

She cleaned the wound. "I'm going insert a drain tube and give it a stitch or two."

She took her suture kit out of her bag, inserted a couple of stitches, and dressed the wound.

"Let me look at that hand," she said to me.

I held out my hand. "Looks ugly. I'm going to have to cut into it."

She made a half-inch cut to expose the wood. Pulling the forceps, I winced in pain. It didn't budge, and the bloody forceps slipped off. She cut again and worked the forceps deeper in.

"You have to help me. Hold your hand down with the other one."

Again, she pulled, and the chunk of wood released its hold. I almost vomited from the pain, and the color drained from my face.

"Splendid job, Doctor," said Norman with a smile.

She looked at Norman, her body soaked in sweat. She dropped her instruments into the boiling water and dove into the sea.

Back on deck, she put on a light long-sleeved shirt and sat down. Norman handed her a cold beer.

She took a swig and looked at Brodie. "What are you going to do now?"

"I have to get these boys back to Managua and it can't be the way they came; the union goons will have that closed off."

"I wish I knew what you were talking about. Lefty's shot up and Tony's hand mangled. Could you please fill me in?" demanded Ally.

Macy nodded toward Brodie. "They have something of value that people are willing to kill for."

Ally asked again, "How are you going to get them out of here?"

"I'll take them down to Bluefield's, then up the Escondido River to Rama. I need to get a hold of John to meet us there."

"Couldn't this cause you a lot of problems?" asked Macy.

"Problems!" Brodie answered. This whole coast is nothing but problems. After a while, that becomes the norm. You don't even realize it is unusual."

"What about the union people; won't they come after you?"

"Not if they know what's good for them. I work with George Morgan. He runs this coast with his seafood plants he put hundreds of Indians to work. If George puts the word out there will be a major uprising. Those union boys won't have a chance."

"What's the plan?" asked Ally again.

"As soon as it gets dark, we'll head for Puerto, I'll hold offshore. Kokie, you take the canoe into the beach, go to the fish plant and tell Carlos to call John in Managua. Tell John we'll meet him in Rama in twenty-four hours after we drop you off. Tell him as much as he needs to know but lay low after that."

Kokie nodded his head.

"Better eat up, it's going to be a long ride," informed Brodie.

We were shocked when Alley added, "I'm going with you."

"You sure?" questioned Brodie.

"Absolutely. Lefty and Tony are my patients. I have to make sure they get somewhere safe."

"That's very kind of you," said Macy.

"Kindness has nothing to do with it. I'm a doctor; that's what I do," she said as she packed up her medical kit.

CHAPTER 32

After a lobster dinner, we set sail under the setting sun. The northeast wind pushed the *Creole Princess* along. Eleven-thirty, in the dark, we lay a mile off Puerto Cabezas. We said goodbye to Kokie as he dropped into the canoe and paddled to shore.

Sailing along, the stars were so bright that one could reach out and touch them. Lefty was in the right bunk in the cabin, under heavy sedation. Ally monitored his condition. Macy and I found a semi-comfortable place on deck when Brodie took the helm so Ona could sleep. Ally poked her head out of the hatchway to look around.

"If it wasn't for the bullshit, I'd be enjoying myself," she yelled back at Brodie.

"Hell, Ally, it's the bullshit that makes it enjoyable," he yelled back.

"If you say so," she laughed. "How much longer?"

"It should be light in an hour. We won't get to the Bluff until the afternoon, so sit back and enjoy yourself," he said as he dropped a line in the water with a fishing lure. Ally ducked below to check Lefty for fever.

"Sounds like Brodie is having a good time," I told Macy.

"Probably breaks the monotony, mate," Macy answered.

I watched Brodie throw a lure into the water, then went back to the cockpit and asked, "What kind of fish are we looking for?"

"Kingfish or Wahoo is the best, but we'll take a Spanish Mackerel if one is lurking around." he answered.

"Have you done much sailing?" Brodie asked.

"A little."

"Want to take the helm?"

"Sure."

"Hold this course, the prevailing wind is always out of the northeast, keep it off the port quarter."

I settled into the helm and apologized, "Sorry we've caused you so much trouble."

"No reason to feel bad, after Korea, this is a breeze."

"I hear you were at the Chosin Reservoir?" I asked.

"Yeah, I was with 2nd Battalion, 7th Marines, surrounded by three divisions of Chinese. Wouldn't have been so bad, except the temperature was thirty degrees below zero." He pointed to the scar on his cheek. "It was so damned cold when I got this it didn't even bleed, it froze up, so maybe that was a good thing."

No sooner had Brodie said that than he turned around and hauled in the fishing line. "Looks like we got one," he said.

"Spanish Mackerel," he said as he hauled the fish on board. "It will make a nice breakfast."

Brodie took out his knife and made a thin cut around the fish's body. He pinched a corner of the skin between the knife and his thumb and peeled off the skin. Flipped the fish over and did the same, then sliced the blade along the backbone to cut out the filets and threw the carcass in the sea without a drop of blood on the deck.

Engrossed as I watched Brodie, I didn't notice Ona standing there holding two cups of coffee. The sun peeked over the horizon.

Ona took the filets forward to cook them up as Ally came up from the cabin.

"I'm worried about Lefty; he is hot. I'm afraid an infection might be setting in. I only have one injection of penicillin, so when we get to Bluefields, I need to get more."

"We're looking at seven or eight hours until we get there. I need to get fuel anyway to get up the river. Will he be safe until then?" Brodie answered.

"The shot I gave him should get him started, but I need to get him on a regimen."

At two o'clock that afternoon, they rounded the Bluff and headed into Bluefields Bay.

CHAPTER 33

Kokie beached the canoe a mile from Puerto at Land Creek. He took the back road home and told his wife he had business to do. When he got there, the fish plant was in full operation, and he asked for Carlos. Carlos returned from taking the divers to the keys and heard there was trouble brewing.

Carlos gave Kokie a hug, "What's up bro?"

"Big trouble, mon."

"Heard about those gringos getting chased. I told them where they were going was dangerous. Where is Brodie now?"

"He's on his way to Rama and wants me to call John Weismann and ask him to meet Brodie there. We need Weismann to pick up Lefty, Tony, Macy and Ally and take them to Managua. Lefty is in bad shape. Could I use your phone?"

"I got his number; I'll give him a call."

Carlos waited as it rang; no answer.

Perplexed, Carlos mentioned Hal Moore.

"John's friend, Hal Moore is collaborating with us to get a decompression chamber. He stays at the Inter-Continental; I'll try there?"

"Sure mon," Kokie replied.

John and Hal were at breakfast together when the clerk brought a phone to their table.

"Hello," Hal answered in his deep voice.

Carlos handed the phone to Kokie, "Mr. Hal, this is Kokie in Puerto."

"Yes, Kokie, what's the pleasure of this call?"

"No pleasure, Mr. Hal, big trouble here. Them union people is chasing gringos. One gringo shot; Brodie is taking them boys to Rama. Lefty, he in bad shape. It is emergency."

"What the hell?" yelled Hal, which got John's attention. "What are they going to do in Rama?"

"What's going on?" asked John inquisitively.

"Here, take the phone. It's Kokie in Puerto."

"Kokie. What's up?"

Kokie explained the situation as John listened intently. He didn't question when he heard Brodie wanted him in Rama.

John hung up and looked at Hal. "Come on; we have to go to Rama."

CHAPTER 34

Rumors of a map to the hidden gold cache had circulated for years; people had seen it with their own eyes. The revolutionary Santiago tasked ten of his most trusted compadres with leaving no stone unturned as they searched for Sandino's map. Torture and murder were not out of the question.

Charlie McCabe knew of the hidden deposits of gold, but unlike Santiago, he had inside information. If anyone knew of the location of the gold, it would be Ed Thompson, who was with Sandino before Somoza assassinated him.

Charlie studied Thompson, aware of his history of fighting with the Marines. Then, he changed sides to fight with Sandino and became part of his inner circle.

Ed Thomson's saga began early on fighting with Sandino. Thompson fell in love with a young revolutionary girl, Carlita. Small in frame, she was fearless, immune to the rigors of revolutionary life, out to prove she could ride, fight, and murder with the best of them. Amid the death and destruction, they were drawn to each other, and from then on, they were together.

When the revolution ended, Thompson and Carlita's lives were in danger due to the revolution. The government considered Thompson a traitor, and a price was on his head. They hid out in a deserted mining camp. Life was bliss for them both. They thrived on this clandestine existence.

Carlita became pregnant. Thompson prepared to deliver their child. Tragically, the delivery went horribly wrong. She gave birth to a healthy boy and began to hemorrhage. She died while she held Thompson's cheek as he helplessly looked down at her.

Unprepared for a child, he had to get help. The only person he trusted was the Moravian Pastor he befriended in Santa Rita. He buried his wife, bundled his newborn son, saddled his horse, and rode hard for Santa Rita. Before he left, he thought of his son's future. He wrote down the treasure's location on an old piece of parchment, rolled it up in a leather cover, and asked the pastor to take it for safekeeping. The pastor never knew what he received and kept the secret locked in the church vault for thirty years.

He left his other treasure, his son, with the pastor. When Thompson arrived, the American missionaries working at the church had adopted the baby. After completing their mission, the couple took the baby back to the United States and raised him as their own.

CHAPTER 35

Charlie set out to find Ed Thompson when he heard the old gringo holed up in a deserted mining camp. Riding his indestructible BSA 250 one-cylinder motorcycle, he began his search.

The once well-maintained road to the mining camp became a series of washout bridges, ravines, and choked overgrown jungle. In places, it was hard to make out the road at all.

The smell of camp smoke stopped him, and he began to reconnoiter on foot with a pistol in hand. Inside the camp, rundown mining equipment lay on the ground. A marker located Carlita's grave.

A tall man pulled a bucket of water up from the well. No doubt this was Thompson.

Thompson didn't notice Charlie until he yelled, "Ed Thompson!"

Thompson jerked around with his heart in his throat and spilled water down his pant leg, "Who are you" he demanded arrogantly.

"Charlie McCabe. We have to talk."

He knew Charlie's reputation and answered, "About what?"

"Sandino's gold."

"Piss off. Get out of here before I rip your liver out, you son of a bitch!"

Charlie pulled out his pistol aimed at Thompson's chest at twenty paces, "You're going to tell me where it is."

"I ain't telling you nothing!" as he swung the full bucket of water and heaved it at Charlie.

The water and bucket came at him. Charlie took a shot and missed.

Thompson heaved a 2-inch metal shaft and hit Charlie in the knee, dislocating his kneecap.

Charlie took another shot and grazed Thompson in the head. Thompson dropped to the ground unconscious.

In excruciating pain, Charlie reached down to shove his kneecap back in place. He dragged his wounded leg and looked over the bloodied Thompson and found he was still breathing. He took a knife out of his boot, cut the rope to the well, and rolled Thompson over. He tied his wrists first, then his wrists to his ankles.

He entered Thompson's sparse one-room cabin to find anything that could give him a lead. Inside was tidy, and the bed was made. A gun belt hung on a nail beside the bed with a .38 silver magnum revolver loaded. Photographs hung on the wall.

On a maple desk with a hutch on top rested an old cigar box. In the box were letters. One old, unsealed envelope, brown with age, caught Charlie's attention. Written on the front, To Carlito, my son. Open after my demise.

He gently opened the back flap to find two separate folded notes that matched the aged envelope. He unfolded one and began to read. It contained no niceties or fatherly affection but to the point.

> *Carlito, after my death, take the accompanying note to the Moravian Church in Santa Rita and present it to the pastor. He will give you a leather-bound package. When you study the contents, you will know what to do.*
>
> *Ed Thompson*

As he unfolded the other note, his kneecap began to throb with pain. Rubbing his swelled knee, he read.

> *To the reigning pastor of the Moravian Church in Santa Rita, present to the bearer of this note Ed Thompson's package placed in the church vault for safekeeping.*
>
> *Respectfully, Ed Thompson*

Thompson moaned out by the well. Charlie slid the notes into his shirt pocket and buttoned the flap.

He ignored the pain in his knee and took Thompson's pistol, went outside, and stood over Thompson as he squirmed on the ground. With the pistol, he went to Thompson's horse and shot it twice in the head. The horse dropped to the ground, kicking its hind leg in a death spasm.

He limped back to his motorcycle and tossed Thompson's pistol in the well.

CHAPTER 36

Dona Alana said her nephew Joaquin was a bad boy. He was as bad as they get. No inner core, no moral inhibitions. He could cut a man's throat and watch him bleed out. The kind of person Santiago looked for.

Joaquin joined up with Santiago, with promises of fame, riches, and glory, to do his dirty work.

Santiago gave Joaquin and two other men the assignment to cover the trails leading into Santa Rita and especially be on the lookout for gringos. They received a license to kill.

A half mile out of town, they set up a camp. Joaquin started a fire as the other two boys went out to hunt for food. As the fire blazed, they came in with a jungle possum they'd shot. Joaquin gutted the possum and tossed it into the fire to let it roast. He checked it now and again with his razor-sharp machete.

Juices ran out of the blackened carcass. Joaquin cut out the hind quarter and held it close to his lips when he heard a motorcycle come down the trail. He told his two companions to get their weapons and then led them up the trail to set an ambush.

Charlie knew the old mule trail that led to Santa Rita. It was slow going and a hard ride, but nothing his BSA couldn't manage. As he got close to Santa Rita, he smelled roasted meat and knew he wasn't alone on this trail. He stopped to check his weapon and tucked it under his belt. He wasn't going to take any chances. He advanced in a heightened state of awareness.

Joaquin and his two men stood concealed off the trail to spring their ambush. Charlie got within ten yards. They stepped out on the trail and pointed their weapons directly at Charlie.

"ALTO!" Joaquin yelled.

Charlie McCabe looked as gringo as they came. He stopped and knew he was in trouble. He made a quick decision, fight or flight. He decided to do both.

"Levanta tus manos!" Joaquin commanded.

Charlie steadied the bike, raised his hands palms forward, and placed a big smile on his face. He looked directly into Joaquin's eyes. The big smile caught Joaquin off guard, which gave Charlie more time.

Locked on to Joaquin's eyes, he pointed down to his stomach.

Joaquin and his two men looked confused. Charlie slowly moved his right hand down to his stomach and gestured with his left that he had something for Joaquin. His hand went below the handlebars out of sight, and he took hold of the pistol.

Joaquin was tough and mean, willing to kill for no reason, but he had one flaw... he couldn't shoot a firearm worth a damn.

Charlie quickly brought up his pistol to fire. Joaquin saw the pistol and, in a panic, fired his gun. He missed by a wide margin, but Charlie didn't. The first round plugged Joaquin in the heart, and it killed him instantly. The other two men hit the ground to dodge Charlie's rapid fire.

Taking advantage of their fear, Charlie grabbed his handlebars, put the bike in gear, laid it over, gunned the engine to spin a one-eighty, and raced back down the trail. He'd have to figure out another way to retrieve the package from the Moravian Church in Santa Rita.

Charlie blew his cover in the gunfight with Joaquin.

Santiago learned about Charlie and the ambush. He assumed Charlie knew the location of Sandino's map.

Thompson regained consciousness and didn't know what hit him. He had no memory of the trauma. The last thing he remembered was pulling the bucket from the well.

His head hurt, and he couldn't see due to the blood caked on his face. He tried to wipe his face but couldn't understand why he couldn't move his arms or legs tethered around his back. He felt the rope around his wrists with his fingers. Panic set in as he violently pulled on the ropes with arms and legs to free himself.

Deep guttural sounds came out of Thompson's mouth. He finally settled down and felt the knot tightly cinched at his ankles. He worked the knot; it took over an hour to free himself.

He lifted himself up and allowed the cobwebs of his mind to clear. How did he get the wound on his head? He tried to remember, but his mind was blank.

Thompson looked around and saw his dead horse. He stumbled into the cabin; his missing pistol was the only thing out of place. He was in danger and needed help. He decided to sneak into Waspam and hole up with the Chinese lady and her daughter until he figured out what to do next. Once on the main road, he flagged down a truck and hitched a ride to Waspam. It was a three-hour ride, and he slept all the way.

The gun battle with Santiago's men ruined Charlie's chances of getting the map. Back in Puerto, while he ate dinner at the Malecon, he overheard Brodie talking about going up the Coco to look for gold. He found another opportunity to get the map. Elated to have closed the deal to get the package for a mere five thousand dollars, he clandestinely followed to make sure the map was secure.

In the dark shadows of the streets in Waspam, Charlie watched the conversation between Tony, Macy, and Lefty inside the Chinese Restaurant. Thompson hurried into an open, darkened field. He didn't notice Charlie standing in a dark corner near the restaurant. In these river towns, a shot would ring out, and no one would take notice.

Shot through the head, Thompson dropped to his knees and fell on his face, where he bled out amongst the cow dung in the dark field. It wasn't until the morning light that someone found his lifeless body, already surrounded by Nicaraguan turkey buzzards.

CHAPTER 37

The *Creole Princess* approached the fuel dock in Bluefields. The waterfront was a collage of multi-colored wooden structures precariously perched on the overhang of the bay.

Brodie instructed Macy and me, "You two lay low while we're here. Word travels fast on the coast. We'll motor from here up to Rama. I want to get going as soon as we can. As soon as we get out of Bluefields, we can relax."

Ally went to find a pharmacy while Ona furled the sails.

Brodie was going on blind faith that Kokie called John and that John would be in Rama to meet them.

Ally took less than forty-five minutes to do her medical shopping. Fortunately, in Nicaragua, one could find drugs on the open market. Stocked with antibiotics, the *Princess* headed up the Rio Escondido towards Rama.

John and Hal were aware of the situation Brodie and we were in. They knew Santiago and his men were on the hunt, and no road would be safe. Before leaving for Rama, John and Hal stopped at the Flor de Cana Distillery. Marcos Franciaco, the owner, was one of John's best friends.

"Marcos," John said as he sat down in front of Marco's desk. "I need a big favor."

"What can I do for you, my friend?"

"I need to borrow one of your delivery vans with a big 'Flor de Cana' logo painted on the side."

"That's a funny request. Do you mind if I ask why you need it?"

"Hal and I are on a big story and we need to go to Rama, it would be best if we went disguised as Flor de Cana representatives."

"Of course you can take a van. In fact, to validate your cover, you can make a delivery for me," he offered.

On the outskirts of Managua, heading for Rama, Hal mentioned, "You know, we are no longer reporting on a story; we're now part of the story."

"Yes, but there is something about that package that's intriguing. This could be bigger than a newspaper story," John answered.

"What happens when we get to Rama, and they're not there?" asked Hal.

"We have to go look for them. You know people in Rama, don't you?"

"I covered their baseball team when they were undefeated last year. The mayor and I became good friends."

"Then you'd know someone with a boat and motor?"

"That wouldn't be a problem. You're thinking of heading down the river to find them?"

"Brodie's boat would be a red flag. It would be better to intercept them on a skiff at night," John answered.

The *Creole Princess* motored up the Escondido, a beautiful sight. Thick walls of overhanging jungle pass by as Brodie rigged a tarp over the boom to shade us from the sun.

From inside the cabin, Lefty yelled, "Hey somebody come help me get out of here, It's claustrophobic in here!"

Macy and I looked at Ally. "Yeah, help him out. The fresh air will do him good. The penicillin must be working."

Lefty grimaced in pain as we lifted him to the deck. "Hey Brodie, do you have any more of that special powder?"

"You better hold off that powder. Save it for when you really need it."

"Any chance of a swim to wash off this salt, mate? My hair feels like cardboard." Macy asked.

"It's not a good idea," Brodie said. "Bull sharks work their way up here, so you'd best use a bucket."

We doused each other with fresh water. "Don't get your hand wet," Ally instructed Tony.

I held up my hand. "Will this work?"

"Yes. Just don't get it wet. I don't want an infection to set in."

When we finished, Ally took a bucket and a rag and washed Lefty the best she could. "I could get used to this," said Lefty, giving Ally a big smile.

"Don't get any ideas, if you weren't my patient, I wouldn't give you the time of day," Ally snapped back.

"Hey, Brodie, how much longer until we get where we're going, so I can get a real doctor?" Lefty cried out.

"You won't find a better doctor than the one you got, and you better take it easy on her."

"Take it easy on her! Didn't you hear what she just said to me? She is worse than a viper."

Ally slapped Lefty's wound, and he yelled out in pain. "You'll find out what a real viper I am if you keep fucking with me."

"All right, all right, Jesus!" hollered Lefty. "Is there a beer around? Christ almighty!"

CHAPTER 38

John and Hal arrived at Rama late in the afternoon. The Escondido River was deep enough for small freighters to travel up, which made Rama a prosperous, mid-size port town. Along with the prosperity came the other elements of a port town, which included smuggling, drunkenness, prostitution, and occasional violence. The seedy bars along the waterfront that accommodated the prostitutes were notorious for fights, murder, and mayhem.

John and Hal went to the waterfront and looked for the *Creole Princess*, but she wasn't there.

They dropped off the rum shipment at the Flor de Cana distribution warehouse and bought a case of rum from the distributor. When they found the mayor at his home, they knew the value of offering a bottle of rum to close the deal.

The mayor was glad to see Hal and invited him in. Hal held out two bottles of Flor de Cana, which the mayor gratefully accepted. The conversation centered around the next baseball season and the mayor's high hopes for another undefeated season.

Hal carefully changed the conversation to their urgent need for a boat and motor. He said they were on assignment to write a story about the Escondido River. The mayor, willing to accommodate them, offered Hal and John his personal boat.

As the sun was about to drop, a storm rolled over Rama with fierce winds, thunder, and lightning, followed by a torrential downpour. It was best to wait until the morning, and they checked into the Magic Night Hotel for the night.

Two hours further down the river, Brodie saw the same storm at a distance. He'd been in these storms before and looked for shelter. A creek on the right entered the Escondido with enough water to float the *Princess*.

"A massive storm is about to come. We'll secure the boat in that creek," Brodie informed us.

He maneuvered into the creek, jumped in the water with two lines, and made for the port shore. The lines were secured to tree trunks. We pulled the boat to the center of the stream and tied off the lines, fore and aft.

While he rolled up the awning, the storm struck with fury and blew at more than fifty knots. Brodie and Ona stayed on deck while we took shelter in the cabin. Small tree branches broke off and plummeted to the deck.

It rained with such velocity that we couldn't see the shoreline as lightning cracked around us. A lightning bolt shattered a large tree, causing it to fall across the mouth of the creek.

The storm ended abruptly. Brodie flashed the light at the stern and saw no way out. We were trapped.

CHAPTER 39

On the river bank, Charlie nursed his wounded shoulder and caught a bus to Tegucigalpa. He went directly to the US Embassy. Once past security, he entered the office of Col. Kent Steen, the military attaché.

The first words out of Col. Steen's mouth were, "Did you get it?"

Charlie, visibly perturbed, answered, "No, I didn't get it."

"Why not?" Col. Steen shouted.

"I got shot in the shoulder, but I know who has it."

Steen looked at Charlie's wound, "You know who has it. How do we get it?"

Steen went to the phone and hit the button to call an office staffer. "Blanche, send the medical staff up to my office right away." He hung up and said, "OK, start from the beginning."

The medical staff came in and started to work on Charlie. "We need to get him down to the dispensary."

"As soon as he finishes his report," countered Steen.

"He has lost a lot of blood, Colonel," the doctor insisted.

"All right, goddamn it. He'll come as soon as we finish! Now, get out!" screamed Steen.

Charlie finished the story of his standoff with Lefty and how they left him there on the bank of the river with Lefty retaining the package.

"Where do we find this guy?" demanded Steen.

"If Santiago hasn't captured them, and they make it out of there, I'm pretty sure they will end up in Managua at John Weissman's office."

"Why John Weissman's office?"

"He's the one who sent them out there."

"We need to make sure they make it to Weissman's office."

Steen picked up the phone again. "Blanche put a call into George Morgan's office on Corn Island." Looking at Charlie. "George knows everything going on along the coast and he'll know where they are."

George Morgan assisted the US Fisheries Department and Medi Pesca (the Nicaraguan fisheries department) in Managua. In addition to running his own seafood plants, he organized US fishing fleets that wanted to fish along Nicaragua's Atlantic Coast.

Morgan didn't want union organizers interfering with his operation (or any enterprise in the Miskito region). Morgan was a key asset for the US Embassy in Managua.

After Charlie finished, the colonel had an assistant accompany Charlie to the dispensary to have his wound treated.

"Hello George, Colonel Steen here in Honduras. Thanks for taking my call."

"Colonel Steen, I know why you are calling. The three gringos, right?"

"That's right, what do you have on them?"

"One shot in the leg near Sandy Bay by the union people. Brodie West picked them up and took them to Rama on his sailboat. John Weissman is to pick them up there."

"Look George, we might need your help. Those people have something that is very important. We need to make sure the package gets to Managua."

"I understand. You must know the situation here is very dangerous. Armed conflict could start any minute and people will be in the cross fire."

"That's a possibility, but if the other side gets the package, more people will be in the cross fire. Do you have people with guns who can make sure the package gets to Managua?"

"I have those people, but it will take time to organize it."

"Thank you, George. Oh, and George, please let me know if you get any news on Brodie West."

"Will do."

CHAPTER 40

From his headquarters in Rosita, Santiago was informed that the red sails were not seen in Puerto but were seen out at the Miskito Keys. When Santiago heard his henchmen were thwarted by a red-sailed, black boat with heavy firepower, no less, he was furious. He told his collaborators up and down the coast to arm up and be on the lookout for the red sails, and he himself would join the hunt.

From his headquarters in Rosita, Santiago informed us that the red sails had not been seen in Puerto. Still, they were seen in the Miskito Keys. It didn't take long to figure out that the *Creole Princess* was headed for Bluefields to get up the river to Rama.

Santiago left Rosita with three of his men for Rama, and John and Hal left Managua at the same time.

Santiago anticipated a fight and brought military assault rifles and standoff weapons.

CHAPTER 41

At first light, Brodie stared at the tree that blocked the creek.

"What do we do now?" asked Macy.

"Start cutting," answered Brodie as he took out machetes from his toolbox.

At the same time, John and Hal were ready to crank up the engine of the mayor's boat. Hal noticed another boat leaving with four heavily armed men in it.

"You think they are going hunting?" asked Hal.

John watched silently for a moment and allowed the other boat to separate.

"I would assume they're looking for the same thing we are."

As Brodie hacked off big branches, he heard the faint sound of an outboard motor upriver. He wouldn't take any chances and motioned for Ona to bring him the Browning.

He told us to take cover while he got behind the tree trunk and sighted in on the coming boat. The boat passed by and didn't notice them hidden in the creek. Brodie noticed the weapons they carried as they raced by.

Brodie relaxed his grip on the BAR while another boat came with two people in it and aimed the BAR at them. Hal was on the helm as they passed. Out of the corner of his eye, John saw a clean vertical mast among the leafy green jungle and motioned for Hal to turn around.

Brodie recognized John's red hair and Hal's journalist vest as they approached. He stood up and waved them in.

After a short greeting, they got down to business. "How did you get in there?" asked Hal.

"Came in here to get out of that storm last night and this tree fell during the storm."

"It's going to take a chainsaw to get you out of there?" Hal said.

"You have one?"

"No, not right now, but we can get one," said Hal.

John asked, "How's Lefty doing?"

"He's in rough shape."

"Does he have the package?"

"He has, but won't let anybody near it."

"We'll take them and Ally into Rama. There are people looking for you, and they aren't going to be helpful," said John.

"We don't have any other choice. Ona and I will stay here and lay low for a couple of days. When you get to Rama ask someone you trust to come cut us out."

"We'd like to hang around and visit, but we better get a move on," Hal said.

"Quicker the better," answered Brodie.

We struggled to get Lefty to the other boat; it was no easy task. We lifted him out of the *Creole Princess*, carried him down the muddy bank, hoisted him over the tree, and finally eased him into the boat.

Once we were in the other boat, I looked at Brodie. "We don't know how we can ever thank you?"

"No use thanking me now, your asses aren't out of the fire yet. Send me a Christmas card once you get back to the States. Right now, get your butts going."

"You better camouflage that mast!" Hal yelled while he pulled away.

We discussed our plans and knew the Union boys were looking for us on the river and more of them back in Rama.

Hal's idea was to go into Rama in full sight and stay around people so the Union boys couldn't get to us. It was a bit gutsy, but it was our best choice.

Twenty minutes out from Rama, two boats rushed towards us. If it was our adversary, the game was over. We anxiously watched the boats make a big sweeping turn and come alongside. The men in the boats heavily armed didn't calm our nerves.

"Have you seen Brodie West in his sailboat?" one of the men asked.

"Why are you asking?" John answered.

"George Morgan asked us to make sure he made it safely to Rama."

Help had arrived.

"Brodie is trapped in a creek down river, but we have his cargo," John answered.

One of the boats left to look for Brodie and give him support. Hal told them, "Wave a white flag or you might get shot."

We arrived at Rama, where the mayor and a small crowd waited. We figured Union boys were watching in the background. Townspeople helped get Lefty onshore and into the back of the Flor de Cana truck. Ally tended to his needs and made him as comfortable as possible, then gave him a small dose of opium.

The mayor pointed to men inside a single-axle dump truck. "These people will escort you to Managua," he said.

Hal laughed when he saw the dump truck. "Is that the best vehicle you have? It might be a little uncomfortable for those riding in the back."

"These people are used to it, besides, we need to get it back to Managua."

CHAPTER 42

Santiago and his people in Rama were ready. Unaware of the arrangements made to give John and us an escort, they set up an ambush.

Six armed Miskitos with rifles were in the back of the dump truck as we said goodbye. Hal handed another bottle of rum to the mayor. The small convoy rolled out of town, confident the worst was over.

John ensured the dump truck was behind us, but as we traveled along, he got intrigued as he listened to our tale. Hal scribbled down in his notebook as fast as he could to ensure he got it right and stopped to ask more questions. The slow dump truck fell behind.

John, engrossed in our conversation, didn't notice a group of men with weapons blocking the road. He slammed on his brakes to keep from hitting them.

John played his ploy as Flor de Cana's driver as the men came up to his window.

"What's the problem?" John casually asked, with a smile.

"We need to look inside," one of the shooters demanded.

John stalled for time. "We're empty, returning from Rama."

Santiago pointed his pistol in John's face, "Open up the back!"

"I have to unlock it."

"Get the fuck out and unlock it then!"

John got out of the truck and walked back as the dump truck rapidly approached. The driver of the dump truck realized what was happening and laid on the air horn as the armed escorts moved to the front of the dump bed and pointed their weapons at the ambushers.

Santiago was less than six feet away from obtaining his goal. He took John by the back of his neck and placed the muzzle of his pistol on John's temple in a challenge to the escort. After a brief standoff, one of the escorts coolly shot Santiago in the face and splattered his brains over John.

Santiago's days as a union organizer and Sandinista leftist revolutionary were over.

Hal pulled a revolver out of his boot and pointed it at the other ambushers. They were not up for a shootout and ran into the brush. In a state of shock, John stood there, hunched over, head down, arms hung in front of him, covered with brains and blood.

Ally opened the rear door of the delivery truck. "What in the hell is going on!" she yelled as she noticed a headless man lying on the road in a pool of blood. "Oh God," she moaned, then looked at John covered in pieces of brain and blood. "John! Are you okay?" she screamed as she jumped out of the truck.

Hal came around and noticed the carnage. "We need to get out of here."

We led John into the back of the van, still in shock; as Hal took over the driver's seat, Macy sat up front. Hal put his foot on the floor as Ally wiped down John.

"What happened?" Lefty asked in his opioid state.

"One of our Miskito escorts blew a guy's head off," I answered.

"Cool," said Lefty.(Stoned out on opium)

Now, the driver, Hal, took a bottle of rum, opened it with his teeth, took a drink, and passed it to Macy. "Hand this back to John,"

Macy took a drink before he passed it back.

We arrived on the outskirts of Managua at two in the morning. "Go to my mother's house," John instructed.

Hal pulled up in front of a high green metal gate. The house was surrounded by a white wall with broken glass on top. John got out and called for the night guard to open the gate. We drove up the driveway and stopped in front of the covered entryway.

When we entered the house, John called for his mother. She came outside, tied her robe, and turned on the lights.

"What is going on?" she asked, wiping sleep from her eyes.

"I have people with me, and we need to stay here."

She noticed the blood on John's clothes and rushed up to him. "What happened to you, are you hurt?"

"No Mother I'm okay, I'll tell you about it later," he said and turned back toward the door.

"Tell me about it later! Tell me what later?!"

"Mother please, calm down. Come help me bring these people in, one injured."

"Oh my God!" she yelled, following him to the truck.

John opened the truck's rear door as Ally and I looked up in a daze. "Hello Mrs. Weissman, I'm Ally, this is Tony."

"You poor things, please come in.

Hal came around from the driver's side. "Hello Susan."

"Hal," she answered. "You're involved in this? Injured? Oh my God, yes, bring him in."

We carefully laid Lefty down on the couch, and Susan's Texas hospitality kicked in. "You poor things, you must be starving."

"Do you mind if I take a shower," asked Ally.

"Of course not," answered Susan. "Down the hall to the right. I made a big pot of stew. I'll warm it up."

"I need a drink," said John. "How about the rest of you?"

Yes, we nodded.

"Scotch on the rocks?" he asked.

We nodded again.

John poured the drinks, "Tomorrow, after we rest up, I want to go to the office and take photos. It would be nice to know what's in that package?"

"Somehow we have to get Lefty to go along with it."

I took a drink of scotch, "He'll go along with it, or I'll shoot him in the other leg."

CHAPTER 43

The next day, cleaned up and presentable, we lined up against John's office wall for a group photo. Lefty, in the middle, sat on a chair with a bandage around his hip and crutches between his legs. I held up my wounded hand.

"No smiles," John admonished. "We had a rough time of it, I want the photo to show that."

John's photographer took multiple pictures of the group. Satisfied, he left to develop the film and bring back the proofs.

"It's time to see what's in that package," said John.

"I don't want to do that," answered Lefty.

"Why not?" asked Hal.

"It has a higher value than five thousand dollars. If I open it someone may have to produce some more money."

Hal and John looked at each other. "You know we got you back here with your brains intact," answered Hal.

"I have a hole in my leg and the package. Possession is nine-tenths of the law, so I'm in charge here. No money, it stays in my pack."

"How much money are you thinking?" asked John.

While Lefty thought this over, the secretary opened the door to make an announcement. Before she could say anything, two men pushed past her. One was Charlie, with a slight limp, dressed in a yellow suit. The right sleeve hung off his shoulder, and his arm was in a sling. The other was Colonel Steen, dressed in a summer uniform, military campaign ribbons on his chest, and carrying a briefcase.

"Who are you and how did you get in here?" John asked, surprised.

Astonished to see Charlie, "He's Charlie, the assassin," growled Lefty.

Charlie flashed his CIA badge. "You have something that belongs to me," Charlie said as he focused on Lefty.

Lefty had fire in his eyes. "Shit it belongs to you man. You tried to put a bullet in my head. Besides that I've got a better offer, so go fuck yourself!"

Charlie didn't respond. He just stood looking at Lefty with a smirk on his face.

I saw Lefty with that look, which meant he was going in for the kill. "Another thing, you asshole. I know you killed that poor old Ed Thompson."

Charlie shrugged his shoulders. "The coast is a dangerous place; people get killed out there all the time."

"With a .45 in the back of the head!!" Lefty fired back.

"Sometimes with a .45 in the back of the head," Charlie nonchalantly answered.

It was then I knew Lefty had something on Charlie, something big. "You were adopted, weren't you?" Lefty slyly smirked.

With a confused look, Charlie backed up a short step and shot back, "What's that got to do with anything?"

"I'll tell you what it has to do with it, bright eyes. Ed Thompson just so happened to be your father. You blew his fucking brains out!"

Charlie's face lost its color. "Bullshit! How do you know Ed Thompson was my father. You're bluffing, you asshole."

"I'm not bluffing, Charlie. I have proof."

The whole room was stunned by Lefty's revelation. We waited for Lefty to continue.

After a pause, Charlie regained his composure and focused on Lefty's eyes. "Bullshit!" he stammered. "You don't know what you're talking about!"

"I don't, aye? The next time you're in Santa Rita, check with Kokie's uncle. Before he opened his hardware store, he was the pastor of the Moravian Church. He knew your father and took you in after your real mother died. Aren't your adopted parents Bill and Ann McCabe who were summer missionaries in Santa Rita?"

Charlie's eyes continued to burn a hole through Lefty.

Before the situation got any further out of hand, Charlie turned to Colonel Steen. "Let me introduce you to Colonel Steen with the US State Department. He'll explain the situation."

"Lefty, what we think you have is a map where Sandino hid millions of dollars' worth of gold to finance his rebellion," Steen said.

He took a moment to let Lefty absorb what he said, then continued, "The gold belongs to the people of Nicaragua. Our mission is to find the gold to keep it out of the hands of the present socialist movement."

Everyone was quiet. Then, Colonel Steen hesitated, "We are authorized to pay you thirty thousand dollars for that document."

"After what you told us, we can't sell you this document. It belongs, as you say, to the people of Nicaragua," insisted John.

"The offer holds true to inspect the document. If it's what we think it is, we'll notify the proper authorities," Steen continued.

"Thirty thousand dollars isn't enough," Lefty broke in and looked at Ally. "How much does a decompression chamber cost?"

"Eight thousand, four hundred and twenty-seven dollars and forty thee cents," she answered.

"Make it a cool forty grand. Ally needs money to get the decompression chamber out there and set it up; or no deal," answered Lefty.

Ally stared at him. "Is that you talking, cold-hearted Lefty?"

"Well, Ally – you did get me here alive. I do owe you something."

Ally shook her head. "Well, well wonders never cease."

Colonel Steen turned, placed his briefcase on a chair, and opened it. He took out four bundles of hundred-dollar bills and placed them on the table. "Open the package," he said.

Lefty reached into his backpack, pulled out the leather package, and placed it next to the money. With a pocket knife, he cut the knot and gently unrolled the old, stiff leather.

Inside was brown dust. Whatever was in the package had been eaten by termites years ago.

Charlie and Colonel Steen looked at each other, said, "Thank you; that's all we need to see," and turned to leave.

Charlie stopped to glare at Lefty with squinted eyes.

Lefty stared back at him with disdain until Charlie turned and walked away, leaving the room and closing the door behind him.

CHAPTER 44

Weeks later, I sat at the bar in Tony Nik's Café and gently rubbed the still pink scar on my right hand. I sipped Jack Daniel's on the rocks and checked my watch. It was five minutes to three when Lefty entered, assisted by a cane. He limped toward the bar, a spent bullet hung from a gold chain around his neck. Huh, five minutes early, that's a switch.

Jim placed a beer on the bar as Lefty struggled to get up onto the bar stool. Once settled, he gulped down half the bottle and put it on the bar.

"How did your date go yesterday with the plump chick with blue lipstick?" I asked.

"All right, I guess," Lefty answered as he finished the rest of his beer.

"What did you do?"

"Went to the zoo."

"Went to the zoo! Wasn't that hard on your leg?"

"She brought a wheelchair and wheeled me around."

"That's it?"

"That's it," Lefty answered, "That's what she wanted to do."

"That's crazy."

"She's a crazy chick."

"Did she pay you?" I asked.

"Fifty bucks and bought lunch."

"Crazy," I answered.

I shook the ice cubes in my drink, "How did you find out about Charlie?"

"Kokie told me on the way to Sandy Bay."

"That's what you were talking about. I could hear you, but didn't know what you were saying."

"He told me the whole thing. He said Thompson brought in Carlito while a young missionary couple helped his uncle for the summer. When they left, they took Carlito with them and changed his name to Charlie."

"Didn't Thompson know about it," I asked.

"Kokie said he never asked about his son. Didn't seem concerned and his uncle never brought it up. He did say that Thompson helped get the store up and running when he bought the inventory."

"That's weird," I answered.

"I asked why his uncle didn't mention it to Thompson. He said on the river it's always healthier to keep your mouth shut, say the least amount possible."

"We found that out to be true," I answered, sipping my Jack Daniels.

"We sure did," replied Lefty as he gulped his beer.

"Why didn't you tell anybody this before you got to John's office?" I pushed.

"Are you shitting me? I had a bullet hole in my hip and stoned out on opium. I didn't even think about it until Charlie walked into the office."

"We were preoccupied," I nodded and ordered another drink.

After a pause. "Have you heard from Macy?" asked Lefty.

"No, but by now he's pretty familiar with the landscape down there. I'm sure he's doing okay."

"Probably down there looking for that lost treasure," said Lefty.

"Probably," I answered as I rattled the ice cubes in my drink.

Jim brought Lefty another beer.

"You know what Tone?"

"No, what?' I answered.

"I think I'm going to write a book."

"Write a book! Have you ever authored a book?"

"No, but it's a good time to start," Lefty answered.

"What are you going to call this book?"

"I think I'll call it 'Sandino's Gold'."

"Huh?" I answered, puzzled.

ACKNOWLEDGMENTS

First, I want to thank my friends in Nicaragua, who furnished so much fodder for the book. Although the story was fiction, finding them in such real-life situations wouldn't have been a surprise. Their lives and accomplishments were more dynamic than fiction. Thanks, Gang!

Next are my friends, who assessed the waters by reading my earlier drafts. There is Mo Mosby, who told me the book was short on description. Phil Friday didn't like the ending, causing us to re-work it for the better. Kerry Robusto, my Doctor's wife, reads my stuff and has checked in on me from time to time to make sure I'm okay ever since my wife Juliet died.

Then, of course, we can't forget Hal Moore and Wayne McLennan. Hal said I was authentic, but to be honest, Hal has recently passed on and was genuine and remembered.

Wayne is from Australia. Yes, you guessed it. He was Macy and accomplished those things, plus much, much more. He now lives in Amsterdam with his wife, who is an accomplished writer.

Last but not least, I want to thank my readers. It amazes me when someone takes the time to sit down to read one of my books. What amazed me more was when they told me they really enjoyed it. That makes me so happy... Thanks

About the Author

Author Bob Means joined the Marines in the 1960s to escape a troubled childhood. Oblivious to the war in Vietnam, he was soon in the middle of combat, surviving two of the severest operations during the war (Operation Swift and the Tet Offensive). He returned home to struggle with his sanity, suffering from PTSD and an addiction to adrenaline. Bob found relief when he was invited to build an orphanage in Guatemala. This led to a thirty-year adventure as a shelter consultant in overseas disaster relief through a faith-based organization.

His fictional writing is inspired by his travels and the people he met, drawing on their experiences to create his stories. Although his writings are fiction, they are not far from the truth.